Penguin Books
Johnno

David Malouf was born in Brisbane. His father's family came to Australia from Lebanon in the 1880s and his mother's family from London just before the First World War. He was educated at the Brisbane Grammar School and the University of Queensland.

His many awards include the NSW Premier's Award for Fiction for *An Imaginary Life*, the 1982 Melbourne *Age* Book of the Year Award for *Fly Away Peter* (Penguin 1983), and the Gold Medal of the Australian Literature Society for *Neighbours in a Thicket*, a collection of poems, in 1974, and again in 1983 for *Child's Play* and *Fly Away Peter*. In 1985 *Antipodes* was awarded the Vance Palmer Award for Fiction. *Voss*, an opera from the novel of Patrick White with libretto by David Malouf and music by Richard Meale, was first performed in Adelaide in 1986 by the Australian Opera and has since been recorded.

In 1988 he was the first winner of the Pascall Prize for achievement of excellence in creative writing. In 1991 *The Great World* was awarded the Commonwealth Writers' Prize, the Miles Franklin Award and the Prix Femina, and in 1992 the Festival Award for Literature (South Australia).

David Malouf

Johnno

Penguin Books

Penguin Books Australia Ltd
487 Maroondah Highway, P.O. Box 257
Ringwood, Victoria 3134, Australia
Penguin Books Ltd
Harmondsworth, Middlesex, England
Viking Penguin, A Division of Penguin Books USA Inc.
375 Hudson Street, New York, New York 10014, USA
Penguin Books Canada Limited
10 Alcorn Avenue, Toronto, Ontario, Canada M4V 3B2
Penguin Books (N.Z.) Ltd
Cnr Rosedale and Airborne Roads, Albany, Auckland, New Zealand

First published by University of Queensland Press, 1975
Published by Penguin Books Australia, 1976
30 29 28 27 26 25 24 23
Copyright © David Malouf, 1975

Typeset in Journal Roman
Printed and bound in Australia by Australian Print Group

National Library of Australia
Cataloguing-in-Publication data:
Malouf, David, 1934–
Johnno.
First published, St Lucia, Q.: University of
Queensland Press, 1975
ISBN 0 14 004256 3
I. Title

For Carlo Olivieri

I have great comfort from this fellow. Methinks he hath no drowning mark upon him; his complexion is perfect gallows. Stand fast, good Fate, to his hanging! Make the rope of his destiny our cable, for our own doth little advantage. If he be not born to be hanged, our case is miserable.

Shakespeare

Prologue

My father was one of the fittest men I have ever known. A great sportsman in his day, boxer, swimmer, amateur footballer, he was still bull-shouldered and hard even at sixty, though a good deal of his muscle had gone to fat. He didn't drink. He hadn't smoked since a day during the First War when he'd accepted a bet and thrown a whole packet of Capstans over Victoria Bridge. Except for the occasional cold, he had never had a day's illness that I could remember. Two weeks before his death he had been examined for a new insurance policy. When the report arrived, on the morning of his funeral, it declared him to be A1 in every respect.

I was out of the country again on study leave, and the telegram announcing his heart attack caught me in the midst of a whole series of muddles that I had simply to leave where they were, all untidy ends, while I got a plane booking, scraped up the money to pay for it, and started back.

I had expected to find my father dying and the family in a state of shock. Instead they were utterly calm. The first stroke had been followed rapidly by three more and he had died within an hour of my leaving London. The funeral was arranged, notices had been placed in all the papers; there was nothing for me to do. Still dazed after the flight, I stood around shaking hands with people I hardly knew, or sat for long hours with my mother in the big darkened room they had found for her at my sister's. She had refused utterly to go to bed. Propped up with pillows, in a new bed-jacket and gown, she rocked back and forth in the sunlight, and when night came at last, sat up rocking in the dark. I dabbed her temples with a handkerchief soaked in cologne, as she used to do when I was sick as a child, and read her the letters that came flooding in with every post while she rocked and sobbed. With her hair hanging loose and her mouth oddly agape, she would doze off while I was still talking to her, then suddenly jerk awake to remind me, in a thick voice, of some document I must search for that she had just located in her sleep. It was in the cashbox at the bottom of my father's lowboy. Or in one of her dressing-table drawers in a red plastic folder. She prided herself on the fact that she knew where everything was. Everything!

My father's affairs were in a good deal of disorder. Like many self-educated men he had no faith in book-keeping and preferred to keep things in his head. Part of my business over the next week or so would be to gather all the cheque butts, bills, invoices, receipts that covered his dealings over the past seven years and get them into order for the solicitor. It was my mother eventually who would track everything down. It was all there, she kept reassuring me, nothing had ever been thrown away, she would find it all in time. And out of her snatches of sleep she would start up with a new discovery. The deeds of Scarborough! They were in an envelope in her linen press, at the very bottom under the towels, together with a whole lot of other papers from the same period. And in the garage there was a tea-chest full of old files that had come from Edmondstone Street, when we moved after the war. Also, somewhere, a flourbag full of crowns. She couldn't remember where they were for the moment. She'd find them later. Going down to the house again, in her sleep, to rummage through empty rooms. . .

I felt superfluous. In spite of the funeral service and that scorching hour in the cemetery at Toowong (I knew the place well enough, we had gone there every Sunday in my childhood to put new flowers on my grandparents' grave) the reality of my father's death had failed to get through to me. It was my sister's children who seemed closest to feeling as I did in that strangely muted house. Too small to realize quite what had happened, they tiptoed in and out of my mother's room with cups of tea; they hushed their friends as they played on the verandah, watched, asked no questions, were "good". We were all extraordinarily quiet. There were no hysterics. Going about our business in the usual way (my sister even made the little girl a birthday cake), trying not to let it show — this was the style my mother had imposed on us always, a style we thought of as English, as opposed to the emotionalism of my father's people. At the funeral, I remembered painfully, one of his sisters, the older, unmarried one, had wailed and beat the coffin with her fists. I was relieved, after a day or two, when my mother was well enough for me to go down to the house and begin.

It was a strange business, that week of raking through drawers and cupboards at the house — sorting, assembling, burning — and of preparing its rooms, since my mother would never live there, for strangers.

It wasn't the house of my childhood. We had moved there in 1947 when my father built the place, huge, ugly, show-offish, after his own design. I had never really cared for it. My memories were all of our old house in South Brisbane, with its wide latticed verandahs, its. damp mysterious storerooms where sacks of potatoes and salt had been kept in the ever-dark, its washtubs and copper boiler under the porch, its vast garden that ran right through to the street behind, a wilderness that my grandfather, before he died, had transformed into a suburban farmlet, with rows of spinach, tomatoes, lettuce, egg-plants, a shed where onions and garlic hung from rafters, and a wire coop full of fowls. The new house at Hamilton was stuffily and pretentiously over-furnished and depressingly modern. It represented an aspect of my father, of his earliest ambitions perhaps, that I had never understood, some vision of worldly success and splendour that I could find no model for. Victorian armchairs covered with French velvet, bevelled glass mirrors, brocade curtains, chandeliers. The only thing I could connect it with was a set of raw silk bed-covers that he had penpainted for my mother's glory chest. Blazoned all over with red and yellow poppies, the oil paint crusty, the oil seeping into the material with a brownish stain, these objects had always impressed me with their gaudy opulence and seemed all the more extraordinary because my father had painted them at twenty when he was a

4

member of Brisbane's toughest rugby push.

Now as I began to sort through his "effects" it occurred to me how little I had really known him.

Like most sons I suppose, I had forced upon my father the character that fitted most easily with my image of myself; to have had to admit to any complexity in him would have compromised my own. I chose the facts about him that I needed: his one solid gold tooth that glowed when he laughed like a miraculous image in a southern monastery; his habit of crossing himself whenever he passed a church; his talent for walking on his hands along the beach at Scarborough, strutting about like some exotic bird, carrying his body through the air as if it were plumage, heavy, extraordinary. I found these images of him comfortingly foreign. Like his skill at athletics (which I decided early I should never try to equal) and his passion for building things. Wearing a leather apron and shorts, with his tool box open on the bench behind him, all its bits and chisels neatly stacked, and a stub of pencil behind his ear, he would work for long hours in the gloom under the house, planing, sawing, working away with his chisel and mallet at elegant dovetails and grooves. He built us, at one time or another, a caravan, two beach houses with beds that went up into the wall, several monstrous wall units, box-kites, a model sailing boat, a set of swings, and before we abandoned the old house replaced all its cast-iron and venetians with fibro and glass. He had left school at eleven to become a postboy on the Nanango mails and had never, so far as I knew, read a book. All of this was a gap between us and left my notion of my own independence utterly uncompromised. Now suddenly I was not so sure.

Everywhere here there was evidence of a life I had failed to take account of — birthday cards he had sent my mother during their twelve-year courtship (huge boxlike affairs, all padded velvet and handpainted celluloid), letters, sketches, even an old leather diary of 1928 in which he had jotted down, over the years, some of the "facts" that struck him: the population of Madrid in 1957 (the year he and my mother went to Europe), a list of all the paintings and items of furniture in Room 4 of the Wallace Collection, and the dimensions of various rooms he had modernized (provided, that is, with one of his built-in units) when he was buying and selling houses in the suburbs. My mother was right. She had kept *everything*. My father's cashbox when I opened it (we called it a cashbox because it had a combination) was filled with old envelopes dated and stamped containing pretty well every document the family had ever acquired: school reports going back to our first days at primary school, my sister's swimming certificates, a postcard of the *Orsova*, 12,283 tons (the ship my mother had come out on in 1913), a five-shilling share in the Siegfried Line that a provident aunt had sent me for my birthday in 1940, newspaper cuttings of my father's boxing career, all pasted up on crumbling cardboard, the receipt for my grandfather's tombstone — and a whole lot more that I couldn't begin to examine. My mother was one of the great collectors. Her dressing-table was the Library of Alexandria, a suburban V. and A. Just opening its drawers was like stepping back into my earliest childhood. There were the heirlooms I liked to play with, neatly assembled in an ivory case: my grandmother's wedding ring and a tiny garnet broach that I knew from the portrait of her in evening dress over my mother's bed; a blood-stone seal with my grandfather's initials, E. M., and a replica of the anointing-spoon used at the coronation of Edward VII; packets of pins, needles, hooks-and-eyes, buttons, hairpins; and dozens and dozens of Paton and Baldwin pattern books, with photographs of favourite sweaters and cardigans I had once worn and a green knitted suit I remembered my mother in, with huge yellow buttons, vintage 1937; little blue bottles of Evening in Paris and huge ones of Potter and Moore Lavender; haircombs, evening-bags beaded all over with jet, hairnets, a chignon, a spangled snood. I felt like a housebreaker as I tumbled the contents of the drawers on to the carpet — or a grave-robber, stumbling in among the ruins of an abandoned empire.

Each morning, just after nine, I went down to the house as if it was a regular job and began where I had left off the day before, pausing only to eat briefly at midday on the kitchen step.

It was September, and the roughstone terraces with their thickets of tiny white daisies were aswarm with insects. The whole garden sizzled and hummed. Big slow-flying grasshoppers, so heavy they could barely stay airborne, barged across the lawn or lofted over a wall to the hibiscus. The air glittered, and bees were busy in the cups of creepers that were just bursting into flower, cascading over a trellis or choking a fence. Occasionally one of the local cats strolled through on its way to the waste ground next door and sniffed about for scraps; or a big waterbird floated in from the mangroves downriver and perched for a moment on a dahlia stake. Once I saw a good-sized goanna. Deserted for just a fortnight, my father's

7

garden was already half wild. The darkness under the thickening boughs was alive with midges and heavy with the smell of rotting vegetation, jungle-damp and sickeningly sweet.

Upstairs, in the afternoon stillness, I worked through my mother's linen press and moved on to the spare room at the back of the house that had once been mine.

It was years since I had slept there. After my sister married I had used her room, which was bigger, lighter, and had a view; but the double room at the back was still referred to as mine. It was a storeroom now. Suitcases were piled against one wall, a pair of bed-ends and a set of dining-chairs my father had meant to cover were stacked against another, and the built-in cupboards were full of toasters, electric jugs with ragged cords, radiators, blankets, the covers from our car. The only sign of my occupancy was a faded place on the wallpaper where I had once hung a print, and in shelves behind glass, in the smaller of the two rooms, my books, already mouldy with damp.

I emptied the cupboards and took their contents to be burned. The books I packed in a tea-chest to be transported to my sister's.

This was the last room of all, I was almost finished. There was only the desk, which no one had used for fifteen years or more, its drawers so tight with damp that I could barely get them open. The first two were empty anyway. But in the third, under a set of new spring-back folders, was a layer or rubbish that must have lain pretty well undisturbed since my middle years at school. The usual stuff. I took the drawer out and tumbled its contents on the floor: fuel-pellets for a model aeroplane engine, propelling pencils given out free by Dunlop Rubber and Tristrams soft drinks, newspaper photographs (John Winter clearing the bar at the London Olympics), poker dice, a crumbly gum rubber, a compass with a stub of green pencil, a glass cylinder marbled with coloured sands from the North Coast, even a sheaf (neatly folded) of "stories" that I had punched out one holidays on a borrowed Royal. And at the very bottom, still glossy and unyellowed, the Brisbane Grammar School Magazine for 1949.

I let the pages fly under my thumb, and was about to consign it to the pile of junk behind the door when out of a pyramid of regular, black and white faces I was pulled up short by a familiar, unfamiliar smile.

I turned back to the photograph and stared.

The Stillwater Lifesaving Team, looking solid and smug in their black Speedos, had been arranged in two rows in front of the Old Physics Lab. Arms folded to show off their biceps, knees regularly apart, the older boys sat stiffly upright on a form. We younger ones posed cross-legged at their feet. There were two squads of us, junior and senior, with six in each. We used to practice at lunchtime on the front lawn under the trees, one boy kneeling, one boy prone in the grass, taking it in turns to be either drowned-man or handy by-stander: *one, two*, breathing steadily, *in, out*, pushing down hard with hands spread under the shoulderblades up to sixty, then springing to our feet. And there we all were, all twelve of us, with me in the front row left.

But what had caught my eye, and made me turn back and look again, was a small boy at the very edge of the picture, who wasn't staring out like the rest of us into some sort of rectilinear future, but had cocked his head up, away from Mr. Peck's covered tripod, and was staring diagonally out of the frame.

It was Johnno. No mistaking the big, lopsided grin, the oversized head with its Cagney-style middle parting and brilliantine waves. But what puzzled me, and had, I suppose, even more than the oddness of his pose, leapt out from the page and caught my eye, was the. glasses he was wearing. Round gold-rimmed glasses that might have belonged to his grandmother or been a property from an end-of-term play.

Surely they were wrong! Johnno had never worn glasses. I stared at the photograph for a good three minutes, searching my memory for some image of him, bursting in through the door — breathless, late as usual, his socks round his ankles — or swerving dangerously close as he hurled off on his bike; he was as clear in my mind as if he were there. But the glasses, those odd gold-rimmed specs that sat so firmly on the saddle of his nose in the lifesaving photograph, they simply refused to materialize. Either my memory was at fault or the camera, on that particular afternoon, had lied.

I ran my eye along the row of faces and checked my memory against the names below. Carl Reithmuller, Jim Bostock, Bill Braithwaite, Neil Pickup, Colin Smails, Tippy Thompson, Mervyn Deeks — I named every last one of them without fail. My memory, like Johnno's eyesight, was perfect. Twenty-twenty every time. I could see myself paired with each one of those figures, as we stood opposite one another ready to begin, hands on shoulders, heads up. With each of them, that is, except Johnno. And it occurred to me suddenly that he had never been a lifesaver at all. So how had he got into the picture? What was he doing there? I counted. And sure enough, the number was uneven. Johnno made thirteen.

So the camera *had* lied. Or Johnno had. Those glasses, if one could check them, would turn out, I was certain now, to have nothing in the frames. They were a disguise, a deliberate bending of the facts. A trick set up as carefully that afternoon as Mr. Peck's camera, to preserve something other than the truth, and to make someone like me, nearly twenty years later, stop and look again. A joke with a time fuse.

How like him!

I thought of the times he had caught me in just this way in the old days. Clever as I was, cool and un-shockable as I liked to think myself, he had the knack of turning me into a staring idiot, caught without warning as one of his jokes went off bang in my hand or some new piece of outrageousness left me floundering on the sidelines, unable either to follow or turn away. He was always one jump ahead. While we were hanging round corners, sometimes, or peer-ing into bookshop windows (Johnno pretending to be drunker than he was, I pretending as often as not to be more sober), he would suddenly holler over his shoulder at a group of punters exchanging tips in Tattersall's arcade, or a couple of housewives with shopping baskets, "It's all lies!" — then swivel on his heel and stare at me as if *I* had said it.

It was a trick that never failed. I was always left on the kerb, spluttering, red-faced, trying to clear myself or explain.

Twenty years later I am still doing it. The book I always meant to write about Johnno will get written after all. Johnno made sure of that, on an afternoon years back when we barely knew one another, while he was just a cocky schoolboy setting out to sabotage, for pure devilment, a picture he should never have been in, with his eye on — what? One of the tatty grey pigeons that picked up sandwich crumbs in the yard, which had just taken off in a flurry of dust and was passing at eye-level between Mr. Peck's tripod and the roof of the War Memorial Library? Not, surely, on a future biographer!

Still, the fact remains, he had me hooked. As he had, of course, from the beginning. I had been writing my book about Johnno from the moment we met.

I

He was the class madcap. I see him, a smallish boy with bulging blue eyes, mooning at us through the doors of the New Building verandah, while Soapy Allen, our science master, dictates: the uses of isinglass. . .

Johnno has been put outside, and after whistling up and down for a bit with his fists in his pockets, or watching under cupped hands the golfers on the far-off links, he has come back to make faces through the door, exerting what Soapy calls his "malign influence". The glass of the doors is striped with sticking-plaster from the War, and Johnno, his nose flattened against the pane, his eyes rolling, gives a good imitation of a fish in a tank, his mouth rounded, inaudibly gagging, and immediately afterwards of a baboon from the Gardens menagerie. Soapy pretends not to notice. But he is, in fact, as much under Johnno's powerful spell as any one of us. He is a big chalky man with a passion for dangerous experiments. "No, no," he insists, "no magnesium flares today — no pandering to this weakness for sensation!" But in the pocket of his tweed jacket there is always a good-sized roll of something inflammable, and before the lesson is over the room will be fizzing and flashing while he shakes his head and makes little deprecating clicks out of the corner of his mouth.

13

"This isn't science," he murmurs delightedly, "it's the Royal Show. All you boys are interested in is sensation."

He plays the same elaborate game with Johnno, never addressing him in anything but a highflown rhetoric that gives all dealings between them the air of a scene at the theatre. The scene ends, inevitably, with Johnno's exile to the verandah, and Soapy watches out of the corner of his eye while the notes on helium or copper sulphide flow steadily, full-stops commas and all, from his whiteish-grey lips. Johnno is off-stage, but never quite absent. And occasionally, by long-established precedent, he makes a comeback like Banquo's ghost, mouthing eerily through the glass till Soapy opens the door a crack and he makes his formal protest. "I'm as innocent as a milk-white lamb," he'll say, rolling his blue eyes so that the rest of us have to double up in our desks. And Soapy, briefly allowing him a place in his Fourth Form chemistry course: "Then go you forth, little lamb, and separate yourself from these my goats a comma, in a weak solution of hydrochloric acid, full-stop." But Soapy always relents at the last moment and calls him back for the fireworks.

Still, innocence is something Johnno cannot claim. Not seriously. In class he is an endless source of wise-cracks (delivered in a fierce stage whisper) and of noises that he can produce at will from every part of his anatomy, stentorian belches and burps, farting sounds from the armpit, or real farts either wheezily protracted or released in a staccato series, short sharp punctuations of a sleepy afternoon. Gangling at the blackboard, he makes half-witted attempts to solve geometry problems that leave even the master confused. Asked to construe a sentence out of *Noctes Latinae* he sighs, scratches his head, shuffles from foot to foot and suddenly discovers the most improbable and suggestive translation. Out of class, with the help of a boy whose father is a bookmaker, he runs the school's most profitable SP racket, with half a dozen bullies to beat sixpences out of those who can't pay; and at Cadet Camp organizes "sessions" in the showers at which he wins over three pounds by being able to come faster and further and more often than any other boy in his platoon. Twice in our second year he is theatened with expulsion; once for shop-lifting from Woolworths and once for spiking one of the rowing eights. And on each occasion his mother appears wearing black gloves and a hat and the headmaster lets him off. The prediction is that he will fail the Junior, lose his scholarship and be sent to work at a tyre factory, or be apprenticed to the printing trade, though why these particular careers should be mapped out for him nobody knows. Perhaps the tyre factory is related, somehow, to the french letters he peddles to boys in the Fifth and Sixth, with the sage advice that you should never be without one just in case.

We were all awed, I think, by his sheer recklessness. He would do *anything*. Get up with a shrug of his shoulders and accept any dare. Accept with the same lift of his shoulders any punishment. No other boy in the school appeared so regularly on detention lists or made so many trips across the gravel to the Office.

"He's crazy," people said. "Someone dropped him when he was a baby."

"He's a clown."

"He's a ratbag."

"He'll end up on the end of a rope."

"He's anti-social."

And it was true he had no sense of responsibility, no school spirit, no loyalty to his country or to his House, no respect for anything as far as we could see. It meant nothing to him that minor servants of the British Raj had sent their sons to be educated here in the years before the Great War, or that a tree had been planted in the grounds by a Royal Duke, the son of Queen Victoria, or that the honour-boards in the Great Hall carried the names of seven generals, nine judges of the Supreme Court and a governor of Queensland, not to mention the war dead, whose names were recited, alphabetically, to the assembled school on Anzac Day. Johnno cared for nothing and nobody. No crime was beyond him. He was a born liar and an elegant shoplifter, who could walk through Woolworths at a steady pace and emerge with his shirt fairly bulging with model cars, pencil sharpeners, rubbers, exercise books, wind-up teddy-bears, toy trumpets — anything you liked to name. It was generally agreed he would have slept with his sister if he'd had one. We were appalled and delighted by him. He gave our class, which was otherwise noted only for its high standards of scholarship, a dash of criminal distinction.

His attitude to us was one of unconcealed contempt. We were a lot of "pikers". And he had the same contempt, even less concealed, for the gang of slavish and dimwitted followers who repeated his wisecracks, wore their hair with the same gangster parting, and greeted his every gesture with boisterous guffaws. Johnno was never to be seen without at least one of them in tow: Stal Henderson, whose father

16

owned a property in the west and whose nickname derived from a boast he had made in the first year of having serviced his father's mare; Carl Reithmuller, with his pockets full of frenchies ("as thin as a shadow, as strong as an ox") and the starting price for the midweek races; and The Mango, a skinny crazy-looking kid whose hair stood up all over his head like a sucked mango seed. Johnno took their loyalty for granted and abused them unmercifully. In the middle of a piece of outrageous foolery he would suddenly turn on them and wipe the grin from their faces with a savage: "Piss off, the lot of you. You too Stal! Get lost!" And they'd troop off together like whipped dogs. But ten minutes later they'd be back, trailing along somewhere behind him, giggling, poking one another in the ribs, urging him on. I think now that he hated them. But in those days Johnno and The Boys were to the rest of us — myself included — pretty well indistinguishable. All foul-mouthed, all bullies, all hopeless at French. Johnno was more daring, that's all. If there was anything more to him than that I had no way of perceiving it. I was too busy with the character of Brutus and the boyhood of John Ridd (both of whom, it seemed to me, bore an uncanny resemblance to myself) to see anything more in Johnno than a shameless waster of his own and other people's time and a thoroughly bad influence. Though he was, of course, fun — you couldn't deny that, and our lives would have been poorer without his disorderly presence. But dangerous! It was best to keep out of his way.

II

I had known him longer than the rest. We had been kids together on the beach at Scarborough, and I was stickily embarrassed on my first day at Grammar, just when I had got out of short pants and was preparing, for the second or third time in my life, to put the past behind me and make a good impression, to have Johnno come up and claim me. "Well look who's here," he announced cheerfully, "it's the Professor."

Scarborough was a flimsy bayside settlement on the Peninsula, with Deception Bay and the Glasshouse Mountains on one side and the sandhills of Moreton Island on the other. Each morning at ten the S.S. *Koopa* steamed across the view on the way to Bribie, its two funnels smoking, its silhouette clearly outlined against the blue. At night the light at Cowan Cowan fanned slowly back and forth at the entrance to the bay. Scarborough had one hotel, three shops, and the Ginn's crab kiosk, which sold the sweet pink sandcrabs that could be caught almost anywhere in these waters by sinking nets weighted with a bone. From the beach we would watch the boats making their round of the nets a hundred yards offshore, and sometimes, if we were lucky, one of the Ginn boys would take us out to see them hauled up with three or four blue monsters thrashing about in the mesh and the big knuckle-bone shining clean. In the Ginn's red corrugated-iron shack, with its bare rafters and stamped clay floor, we went sometimes to see the crabs boiled in a vat, throwing their claws in the steamy brackish water while a second load waited in baskets in a corner, one of them suddenly hurling itself out into the sunlight to be chased amid shrieks and caught expertly behind, the long blue nippers, which could take your finger off, working fiercely at the air.

In winter Scarborough was just a fishing village at the end of the line. In summer it was a vast encampment. In the early years of the war, while hostilities were still confined to Europe, and the Royal Navy, not to speak of Singapore, stood firmly between us and any threat of invasion, we had a caravan at Scarborough and would drive down on Friday evenings in our '27 Hup. There was a regular colony of campers on the strip of grass behind the beach and a whole gang of kids who played Donkey on the long wet sands when the tide was out or Cowboys and Indians in "The Trees". Johnno was one of them, and he had been a tearaway even then. One of those wiry, barefoot state-school kids that my mother preferred me not to play with and my father, I suppose, wanted me to be like.

Johnno was what my mother called bad company. "Show me your company," she would recite largely, "and I'll tell you what you are."

I didn't frankly know what I was and I preferred not to think of Johnno as "my company", he wouldn't have had me anyway. But I lined up waiting to be called when they picked teams for Red Rover or Rounders, and slunk off quietly when it became obvious that I would be last. I tagged along when they went out on the dunes with a flashlight to find soldiers and their girls, catcalling along with the rest till someone appeared fumbling with his flybuttons and gave us money to get lost. The Americans arrived early in '42, and we went on frenchie hunts along the cliffs or round the Skating Rink at Redcliffe. You could find as many in a single afternoon these days as the white horses we counted, galloping about in sun-struck paddocks, as we drove down in the car; and I didn't let on that till recently I had thought they were some sort of fungus, hanging shiny and white from the twigs. But I never really belonged to the gangs. I was happiest at home under the tentflaps, reading my favourite Dumas and dreaming myself back into that marvellous Olden Days when people wore satin and spoke French and when everything that happened was History. I was very strong on history. Not the terrible history of our own misplaced continent, with Burke and Wills staggering off across the desert or Leichhardt coming to the end of a dotted line somewhere west of Quilpie — but the history that was recounted in the books I bought at Old Neds in Melbourne Street, huge closely printed Victorian volumes that told the story of the Fair Rosamund and the Wars of the Roses, with diagrams of the Plantaganet family branching out across two pages in marriages and remarriages more interesting than our own family's decent and regular line-up of uncles and aunts, and vastly more demanding of my schoolboy memory than the first four governors.

Australia was familiar and boring. Now was just days, and events in *The Courier-Mail* — even when those events were the Second World War. History was The Past. I had just missed out on it. There was nothing in our own little lives that was worth recording, nothing to distinguish one day of splashing about in the heavy, warm water inside the reef from the next. Only the appearance once of a turtle, stranded at the bottom of one of the red-soil cliffs. And an afternoon of panic, after Singapore had fallen at last and invasion wasn't at all improbable, when we saw what we thought was a Japanese sub lurking in the shallows — though it turned our later to be a petrol tank jettisoned from a passing plane. In the evening the lamp had to be pumped. In the morning there was water to be fetched, in a kerosene tin, from the tank at the top of the hill. Between there were just days. Nothing extraordinary happened.

During these early years at Scarborough Johnno's father was away with the army. In Greece at first, then later in Malaya, where he was posted as "missing" — one of that vast company of fathers, cousins, friends, who had gone off in the early months of the war (I recall being taken on my father's shoulders to see the buff-coloured feathers of the Light Horse go bouncing down Queen Street) and had simply disappeared. They weren't dead. No one believed that. They were "missing". And they stayed missing through all the years at primary school when I was discovering America and the Spice Route to the Indies; through the Age of Elizabeth when the great houses, out of compliment to her, were built in the shape of an E like Queensland state schools; through the days of petrol coupons that put our car on blocks; and through nine hundred episodes of the *Search for the Golden Boomerang*. Till in the weeks after Hiroshima they drifted back into our Victory Polka and Mairzy Dotes world, so wraithlike and thin,

21

so unlike anyone we had ever seen before, that it was better not to ask after them.

Johnno's father was one of those who stayed missing. And the reason for Johnno's wildness, it was universally agreed, was that he was a war child. In the years when it really matters he had lacked the benefit of a restraining hand.

Our own father was too old for the war, so we did have the benefit of his restraining hand. Though I should add that he seldom raised it.

Was I a war child, I sometimes asked. Was there anyone in those days who was not? "Before the war" was a hazy, rose-coloured period I could only vaguely recall. I associated it with the smell of oil-cloth picture books and the little spring chickens we used to eat, a whole chicken on each plate so that everyone had a wishbone. It was simply the earliest things I could remember. The clop of the milkman's horse in Edmondstone Street just before dawn, and our blue-ringed jugs on the doorstep, their crochet covers weighted round the border with Reckitts-blue beads. Or waiting out front for the iceman to come with his hook, and the huge block dripping all over Cassie's floor. Was it the war, I wondered afterwards, or some change in me, that made everything in the years before I went to school seem different from the khaki and camouflage years that came after, when even the flowers we made out of plasticine were a uniform grey, the result of a dozen colours that could not be replaced being patted and squeezed into a single colour that was like the dirt-rolls in your palm. Was it only the war that made things change? And what *would* happen when the war was over? I knew the lights would come on again, all over the world. Even in Queen Street. But what else? What else? I think I expected some miraculous transformation might take place in us, as extraordinary perhaps as the explosion of a row of allied flags out of an empty sleeve (I had seen that at the Cremorne Theatre one Saturday matinee) and I longed for it painfully. The end of the war! Would it come when I was eight, ten, thirteen? I dreamed of it, impatient with the present, fearful of being disappointed, as one dreams of growing up.

Meanwhile, for the duration, we had the war itself. Our spare room at the back of the house, which had once contained nothing but the piano where we sang in the evening and my mother's sewing machine, was hung now with enormous wall-maps that came with *The Courier-Mail.* Here, day by day, we followed the fortunes of the campaign in North Africa, the landings in Italy, the long-drawn-out Russian campaign, and when D-day came at last the plunge out of Cherbourg into the German heartland. Places that would otherwise never have swum into my head have retained even today a spooky fascination for me. Benghazi, Byelograd, Bataan, Kokoda, Anzio, Wake Island. I knew the sea route to Archangel and the name of every U-boat in the German navy, and would have recognized, had they appeared overhead, any plane in the Imperial Japanese airforce — not to mention our own Spitfires, Sunderlands, Hurricanes, Mosquitos, Catalinas, Lockheed Lightings. As well as the wall-maps, and the silhouettes of war planes and battleships, our spare room had a plaster mask of Winston Churchill, complete with detachable cigar, a poem people were fond of at the time called "The Fuzzy Wuzzy Angels of the Owen Stanley Track", newspaper portraits in colour of Stalin, Roosevelt, and Chiang Kai-shek, and a diorama of the evacuation from Dunkirk, which an uncle of my mother's had commissioned and exhibited for the Red Cross. In this miniature war museum we listened to the evening news and my father, before setting out to inspect the blackout, plotted a new landing or salient with wall tacks in scarlet and black. If something really shattering occurred, and especially if there was an unscheduled news flash, my Aunt Vera came up from two doors away and shouted to us from the foot of the stairs:

"Have you heard the news? Isn't it terrible!"

The sudden swoop of her voice at breakfast, or during my mother's afternoon nap, was a sure sign of disaster. "My God," my mother would say, "that's Vera. I wonder what they've done now." And sure enough, the Germans were at Leningrad, Guadalcanal had been taken, the *Centaur* was lost, or some figure we thought of as almost in the family was listed in the latest raids.

I see myself sitting at school one morning, aged six. I am sobbing bitterly. "What's the matter? Why are you crying?" one of my schoolfriends asks, settling beside me on the little form and putting his arm across my shoulder. I look shocked. "Haven't you heard?" I say melodramatically. "BELGIUM'S FALLEN."

It was a catastrophe that had thrown our whole house into confusion just before I left. I thought of Belgium as being rather like Humpty Dumpty. Obviously it could never be put together again, and in

24

this case the wicked king and his men didn't even want it to be.

But the war for me had a private and more sinister dimension. Though I knew with one half of me that it belonged to the world of daylight reality, the world of newspaper headlines and apocalytic announcements from the bottom of the stairs, I also knew, in some other part of my being, that this was only half the truth; there was more to the war than the wavering voices told us, more even than my Aunt Vera knew. When I crawled into bed at night and my father came to put out the light the war took on its *real* form. Giant staghorns leapt through the papered glare of my bedroom window, and our fernery beyond, with its mossy fish-pond and slatted frames hung with baskets of hare's foot and maidenhair, sprang up in shadow around me, an insubstantial jungle there was no way through. I choked. Hitler and Mussolini, those historical bogeymen that even adults believed in, burst in upon me bearing their terrible paraphernalia of barbed wire, bayonets, tin helmets, hand grenades; their purpose now having nothing to do with the wall-map and its pins in our spare room, but being, quite simply, to reach up over the foot of my bed or down over the pillow and drag me into the pallid, black-and-white world of newspaper photographs and newsreels — a world without colour, like the night itself, in which everyone was a victim, pale, luminous, with flesh already frazzled round the edge, and where being a child with curly hair and apple cheeks that everyone wondered at was no protection at all. The war wasn't one of those activities that were strictly for grown-ups. The newsreels were full of children no older than myself climbing up gangplanks

25

or being herded into trains. And how else did they get into the war (I couldn't imagine their parents *allowing* them to go) unless they had been dragged there, over the pillow and down into the furballed, spider-crawling darkness under their beds?

In later years my night terrors came to seem truer to the real history of our times, as it was finally revealed to us, than the list of sinkings and beach-heads that made up the headline news. And it was for this reason perhaps that the explosion of the real war into our hemisphere seems in retrospect like the beginning of a lighter period of my childhood. The war came into the open at last. The Japanese struck Pearl Harbour, and my father took me one brilliant morning to see the first American warships come grandly upriver and swing at anchor off Newstead Park. What I remember is the whiteness of the sailors' uniforms as they stood in dazzling rows on the deck, and the light of that moment floods all the years ahead. There was greater danger of course. But danger is open and easy to deal with. Better any day than dread. The war, now that it was with us, turned out to be quite an exciting affair. A bit frightening at times, but mostly comic and commonplace.

We were given air-raid kits that we took to school with us. They contained rubber mouthpieces that we were to bite on during the raids and rolls of bandage that got used almost as soon as they were given out for bloody knees. My father was made Senior A.R.P. Warden for South Brisbane. He wore a white helmet, a red felt armband, had a gasmask and rattle, and went out each evening after dark to inspect the black-out. Once a week, on Wednesdays, his group came in for their meeting. After practising with the stirrup pump in our back yard, they read through the emergency drill, checked off a list of hospitals, fire-stations, and emergency first-aid centres, and ate a ten o'clock supper of sausage rolls and cream-puffs. Brisbane was suddenly at the centre of things. Though we hardly knew it at the time, our city was having its moment of greatness, its encounter with History: General MacArthur had arrived and the whole Pacific campaign was being directed from his office in the A.M.P. building.

All night now the troop transports rumbled past our house, and in the early dusk, with mosquitos beginning to dance under the bushes and flying foxes in the mango trees tearing into the pulpy fruit, I sat out on our lawn away from the sprinkler and counted them. They went on long after I had run out of numbers, and all through tea and the radio serials I listened to afterwards, and went droning on in my sleep. Neighbours began to evacuate to places like Coonabarabran, and the big houses along the park, where I used to play in the afternoon, were boarded up with chains on the gate or turned over to the Yanks. When my father decided we should stay put our house was fortified with sandbags and workmen came to dig a trench in our tennis court. It filled with water in the first summer and remained a breeding ground for mosquitoes, and a marvellous setting for our games of Cowboys and Indians, till my sister broke her leg jumping across it and my father had the workmen back to fill it in. On the two occasions when the sirens did go, the shelter had nine inches of muddy water in it, so we sat behind sandbags in the garage, on the running-boards of our huge tanklike convertible, and bit hard on our rubber mouthguards, till after an hour or so of foolish expectancy my mother (who thought bombs had your number on them anyway) led us back into the house.

But our one-storeyed weatherboard wasn't the only one to be fortified. The whole city had taken on the aspect of an armed camp, and there were rumours that when the Japanese landed the whole country to the north would be scorched and abandoned in the Russian manner and a last stand made at Brisbane. We were suddenly in the front line. Concrete pill-boxes appeared in the streets and became places where people "did things" after school, or where children who took sweets from strangers were discovered with their heads cut off — victims (now that all the swaggies and metho drinkers had been drafted) of the negroes who congregated round the Trocadero in Melbourne Street and the brothels along the south side of the bridge. Troop transports rumbled day and night, ferrying soldiers from the Interstate Station, where the New South Wales line ended, to Roma Street, where they would board one of the slow narrow-gauge lines to the north. Anti-aircraft guns were set up on the city's high places and the sky at night was crisscrossed with the shafts of giant search-lights, moving pale among the clouds, creating in the blackout a ghostly reflected light that you could actually read by if you half-opened the venetians. Our sleepy sub-tropical town, with its feathery palm trees and its miles of sprawling weatherboard, was on the news-reels. It was the gateway to that part of The War that was raging all over the islands now, just a thousand miles away. Brisbane had, for a time, the heady atmosphere of a last stopping place before the unknown, and there were service clubs, canteens, big dancehalls like Cloudland and the Troc where girls who might otherwise have been teaching Sunday school were encouraged by the movies they had seen, the hysteria of the times, the words of sentimental Tin Pan Alley tunes, and the mock moonbeams of a many-faceted glass ball that revolved slowly in the ceilings of darkened ballrooms, to give the boys "something to remember" before they were mustered (forever perhaps) into the dawn.

Of course there are some things that even the war could not change.

Any morning at nine-thirty, any afternoon at three, our local postman, Mr. Shultz, a big red-faced man with no teeth, might have been discovered in the little courtyard at the back of my grandmother's shop, sipping tea if it was winter and cold ice-block sarsaparilla if it was summer, while my father's sisters (all three of whom were unmarried) went through his mail bag. Mr. Shultz, his boy scouts hat laid aside, would turn a blind eye, while my aunts, who held the seven streets of his round in a grip that not even the Japanese Empire and all its forces could have broken, kept tally of wedding invitations, engagements, sympathy cards, twenty-firsts, who was being invited, who was not — piling the letters out on to the scrubbed wooden table, sorting them, re-sorting, then carefully piling them back. When they had satisfied themselves that all things in the area were going as expected, Mr. Shultz, in the name of His Majesty's postal services, resumed custody of the mails and went on his way.

Nothing in the universe, one felt, could interfere with rituals like these. Not even censorship and those placards that warned us to say nothing, write nothing, since the enemy was always listening. The life my aunts had established was inviolate. They went to mass in the morning, returned to breakfast, entertained Mr. Shultz, kept an eye on my Uncle Nick (who raced greyhounds and was forever falling asleep on his mattress with a lighted cigarette), cooked enormous meals at a wood range that made their kitchen, at all seasons, like a furnace, had nuns to afternoon tea, went once each year to Melbourne to buy new dresses, never spoke if they could help it to known Protestants and wore much too much rouge on their cheeks. My Uncle Nick was a terrible trial to them. A disgrace in fact. He walked his dogs round the suburb in a singlet and floppy old grey flannels, barefoot. He had a girlfriend called Ada who wore ringlets and was thought to be associated with one of the "houses" in Melbourne Street. Behind the choko vines at the end of the yard he fed his greyhounds gobbets of raw meat and occasionally, illegally, in those days when they still used live hares at the races, a rabbit, whose squeals could be heard two blocks away. Uncle Nick was for all of us a man of blood. He had once been to jail for stabbing an Albanian in a card game. He had also gone to the first war, of course, and had never been the same afterwards.

The war — this war or the last one — was the reason for many things. My Uncle Nick was one of them and Johnno's wildness was another. And there was the sudden fall from grace (which was perfectly inexplicable to me) of several "big girls" at Scarborough who had once minded us for the day or

30

taken us to the pictures at Redcliffe, and were now unrecognizable in their high strapped wedgies and pompadours; they were not to be spoken to. One of them, Colleen, had been a particular favourite of mine and I hadn't been at all jealous when an American sailor or a Marine joined us on the Redcliffe bus and fed me Babe Ruths. Now Colleen was someone I wasn't to go out with, and I associated her fall with jitterbugging, which couples performed in an illuminated boxing ring at Suttons Beach — a spectacle my father forbade us to watch. Jitterbugging was a mystery. So too was Leftkas' fruitshop where we had once bought our vegetables. It was now, overnight, declared "black" — though not surely because it sold fried chickens to the negroes, who were restricted to the south side of the river and whose presence had given our nice, old-fashioned suburb a "bad name". That was yet another effect of the war. South Brisbane, with its big rambling mansions, each one with a tennis court, grass or hard, an orchard of lemon trees and loquats, a vegetable garden, a dung-and-feather chicken house — South Brisbane was finally done for; no-one respectable would ever live there again. It had been ruined. Like our girls. Who had been ruined by the high wages they were paid in munitions factories and by the attentions of foreign servicemen, but most of all by their passion for nylon. Things had gone to pieces. Children had been allowed to run wild under the special conditions of Australia at war, and now there was no holding them.

For all this and a good deal more Johnno was the perfect model, and other parents than mine must have shaken their heads over him and thanked their

stars that *they* weren't responsible for the windows
he broke or the words he shouted at old ladies who
objected to his rattling a stick along their fence. I
hadn't been allowed to run wild of course. If I used
bad words, even the mildest "shut-up", I had my
mouth washed out by Cassie with Lifebuoy soap — or
was, at least, threatened with it. I had been properly
brought up. And I sometimes thought how different
from my own homelife poor Johnno's must be. No
wonder he was so awful. What else could you expect?

My mother, I see now, was reproducing for us her
own orderly childhood as the last of a big family in
pre-war (that is, pre-1914) London — though it was
no different from the life that was lived in other
houses where we went to play in the long evenings
after school.

They were all enormous those houses. Huge one-
storeyed weatherboard mansions that had been
intended for more spacious days, and for larger
families than we could manage, they were only half
lived-in nowadays. Every house had its row of locked
bedrooms on one side of the hall. You could look
into them from long sash windows on the verandah,
and believe (as I was told often enough) that people
had died there — grandmothers, little brothers from
scarlet fever or whooping-cough, bed-ridden uncles
from injuries they had received in the First World
War. The high beds had brass ends with superbly
polished finials and little rows of porcelain balusters.
Lace curtains, a lace coverlet and bolster, a washstand
with doilies and a floral jug-and-basin. And often as
not, as in my grandmother's house, a Sacred Heart of
Jesus over the bed, and on the shelves of the dressing-
table a whole series of extravagant saints among

32

artificial flowers and candles. The kitchens were tiled, with walk-in pantries and an old wood range (for baking) beside a newer gas stove, perhaps an Early Kooka like ours, with its legs in tins of water to keep off ants. One huge room, always at the centre of the house, always darkly panelled and with a picture rail, was never opened except to visitors. Its curtains were kept drawn to preserve the carpets and the genoa velvet lounge chairs from the sun; there were chromium smokers' stands and brass jardinieres full of gladioli; on a heavy sideboard, cut-glass decanters of whisky, brandy, port; and a big central lampshade of silk brocade, with tassels, that gave a smoky gold light.

Such rooms were used only after dark. Daytime visitors were entertained on the front verandah among white cane chairs and potted ferns, and when I went visiting with my mother, this is where we were called in to eat pikelets or pumpkin scones for morning tea from a three-tiered cake stand, and in the afternoon, date slices, anzacs and cream puffs, while the ladies, with a lace fichu at their throat, patted the sweat from their upper lips or fanned themselves with plaited palm. Here, on a cane lounge, my mother and other ladies took their afternoon nap, and here we were settled when we were sick, close enough to the street to take an interest in the passing world of post-men, bakers, icemen and newspaper boys with their shrill whistles, but out of the sun. Here too on warm evenings, with a coil burning to keep off the mosquitoes, we sat after tea, while my father watered the lawn and chatted to neighbours over the swinging chains of the front fence and my mother had one of her "conversations" with Cassie's Jack, who was considered a great expert on world affairs. He was our girl's "young man". In fact he was nearly fifty, a veteran of the First World War where he had lost a lung and a former valet to Sir William McGregor, the Governor of Queensland. These days he worked as a gardener at the local convent and did odd jobs like clearing berries from gutters and pumping out drains. A Dubliner with a marvellous gift of the gab, Cassie's Jack also had a talent for turning clothes-pegs into dolls, squares of silver paper into little jumping beans, and ordinary cotton reels and pins into a machine from which I learned to spin yard after yard of off-white pyjama cord. While Cassie got herself ready in her little room on the side verandah he would delight my mother (or was he boring her, I wonder at this distance?) with one of his rambling disquisitions on the probability of war, and later, when all his worst fears had been fulfilled, on the objectives of tank warfare, bombing, and the second front. On very hot nights, when the family had gone inside to play bridge, I was allowed to come and sleep out on the front verandah — though it scared me to be so close to the garden, with just the cast-iron and venetians between me and the dark.

The front verandah was a free-and-easy world of open living, almost the outdoors. The depths of these old houses were dark and musty with damp. Even on the sunniest afternoons you needed a light in our dining-room, its walls were so thickly varnished, its windows so shadowed by the glossy dark Moreton Bay figs whose fruit attracted the flying-foxes and blocked our guttering. As for the series of little rooms beyond the kitchen where Cassie kept her provisions — great sacks of potatoes, onions, sugar, salt — you needed a torch to go in there: the floorboards were soggy underfoot and there were rats. I hated to be sent in, as I was once or twice each month when Cassie's salt box was empty or her sugar cannister needed filling. But for some reason the dark of the kitchen itself, which opened through a wooden arch into the dining-room, delighted me, it was so cosy and safe — especially on summer afternoons when it stormed and the tin roof thundered under the hail.

Here, usually, I did my homework at the big table with its velvet cover, while Cassie peeled potatoes or shelled peas. Sometimes in earlier days, before the war, my mother and Cassie would take it in turns to read aloud from the old-fasioned novels they liked, while Cassie prepared the tea and my mother darned or wound wool over the backs of chairs. *John Halifax Gentleman, The Channings, David Copperfield, These Old Shades* — they were the first adult books I ever knew. I associate them with the dark, lead-light windows of that room, and with the big two-storeyed glass case where my mother kept her best china, the green-glass jelly moulds that came out only for parties, and the little white-columned temple that had been the decoration on her wedding cake. The world of those novels and our own slow-moving world seemed very close. The Channings were almost like next-door neighbours — and preferable certainly to our real neighbours, whose alcoholic son had fits in the back garden and set fire, eventually, to the garage. It was a world so settled, so rich in routine and ritual, that it seemed impossible then that it should ever suffer disruption. Life was a serious affair. For that reason we had to be strict with ourselves; the rules and regulations were necessary, we needed them —

how else could we discover order and discipline? But there were no punishments. Life itself would take care of that.

And before Hitler and Mussolini leapt on to the scene I knew no terrors, except for the rats in Cassie's pantry, a baboon at the Gardens where we sometimes went for a treat (a sullen, red-eyed creature that played with itself in the most shameful manner, and with no warning would hurl itself screaming against the bars), and a radio serial on 4BC that was, Cassie had told me once (no doubt, "to get rid of me"), about a boy who took rat-bait. I was petrified. We had rat-bait ourselves. My father got it in brown-paper packets from the Council, and spread it about under the house — little squares of pink-and-white like coconut ice. The first spooky notes of the rat-bait theme (actually it was Dvorak's *Humoresque*) would send me fleeing into the yard, where my grand-father, a dark, uncommunicative old man whose whiskers prickled, would be pottering about among his egg-plants and tomato bushes or chasing one of our chooks with an axe. I was scared of him too. He spoke no English and was always grabbing me on the run, sweeping me up into the air and crowing like one of the roosters. But I was even more scared of the fate of that foolish boy who had taken rat-bait and staggered off to die of thirst in one of the drains. I would sit under a lantana bush or in Cassie's garden under the back steps, where she grew waxplants, mint, and big red Christmas lilies whose stalks broke with a snap and were hollow like gun barrels, till I thought the wretched serial was over. Or watch my grandfather at one of his strange rituals: winnowing wheat by tossing it into the air with a shovel or shaking it in golden showers from a sieve, or making white cheese by slapping it from palm to palm. He worked here all day, just beyond our overgrown tennis court, behind a lattice fence. His garden was orderly rows of beans, spinach, tomatoes, with strings of flickering tinsel to keep off the birds, and a lop-sided scarecrow that looked so much like grandfather himself that I went sometimes, after he had gone home, to stare at it and wonder if there weren't two of him. Occasionally I helped him pick the beans. And once or twice after a storm I went out with him into the street to shovel up garden topsoil that had been washed into the gutter. He never once entered our house. Late in the afternoon he would come to the bottom of the back stairs, Cassie's stairs, and shout "Something for you, Missus ... " and go off. On the bottom step, when I went down, there would be a lettuce, with dirt still clinging to its roots, or half a dozen yellow tomatoes, or a couple of egg-fruit. When he died early in the war our garden went wild like every other garden in the street, a wilderness of old grey stakes that crumbled and showed their grain amid six-foot thistles, with occasionally, as a last reminder, a purple bean-flower glowing among the weeds.

The rituals by which my own life was regulated it never occurred to me to doubt. They were so utterly reasonable. When I came in from school I changed out of my good things into a sweater and shorts; hung my uniform in the closet by the bed, put my socks in the washbasket, my shoes in the cleaning cabinet, and was allowed on the back verandah (but never never in the kitchen or any other part of the house itself) either a wedge of Cassie's date slice or two anzacs, with a tumbler of malted milk and an apple to clean my teeth. I didn't shout indoors; I never said "she" (She was the cat's mother); and I never swore. If asked to do a message for a neighbour I never refused of course, but I never accepted payment either, no matter how strongly encouraged; not even an ice-cream out of the change. I ate my vegetables, even horrible silverbeet, without complaint; always washed my hands after the lavatory and never called a shilling a "bob". All these rules and regulations, I was convinced, not only trained you in the best behaviour, they also taught you discipline, and discipline was character-building. Like never taking the day off school unless you were really ill ("Come on now," my mother would say brightly at the first sign of a complaint, "we're not Catholics today, we're Christian Scientists — and there's nothing the matter with us!"). Or skipping the dentist. Or the silverbeet. Doing what you didn't like doing gave you moral backbone, as silverbeet gave you muscle and all that drilling at the dentist's gave you perfect teeth. Moral backbone was what prevented people, when they grew up, from drinking and gambling and getting into debt. Children who lacked discipline grew up spineless and had false teeth.

I don't know when all this came to seem to me anything less than the gospel truth. Or what part Johnno, with his wildness and not the sign of a filling, had to do with my growing scepticism, my defection from the dogma that if what you *didn't* like doing was good for you what you *did* like doing was not.

When I think of myself at thirteen I see a neat, darkly serious, well-brought-up little figure with a straight tie knotted in the conventional manner (my father abominated the Windsor knot), clean nails that I was prevented from biting with bitter aloes, a clear left-hand parting, shirts that Cassie insisted on starching till they were so stiff I could barely move in them, and the air of someone who is too well pleased with himself to be true. I wasn't true, of course. I had too many secrets. One of them was a sense of humour (though I had found as yet no good use for it) and the other was the shrewd suspicion, based on irrefutable personal evidence, that there was more going on under people's clean, well-brushed clothes than the building of muscle by silverbeet. I had begun, secretly, to believe some things and disbelieve others, and I was overwhelmed by the discovery that I had a choice. I was still strong enough on Mister Menzies, Commonwealth Savings Bonds, Stromberg Carlson radiograms, and something I had picked up from Band of Hope meetings on the beach at Scarborough, that even a slave is free under the British flag. But I had lost all faith in Santa Claus (years ago), the power of peroxide in the treatment of warts, was beginning to be shaky about the Catholic Church, and had freed myself, by frequent scientific experimentation, of the absurd notion that touching myself "down there" would make it fall off — though I couldn't entirely discount the possibility, at some later date, of going blind.

Some of my upbringing had begun to wear off. And now that I had stopped being impressed by the honour-boards at school, with their lists of prize-winners and the war dead in indiscriminate gold leaf, I even had some notion of being a rebel. Of sneaking over, as it were, to Johnno's side.

III

It was for this reason, perhaps, that when Johnno asked me one day, in his usual shoulder-shrugging, take-it-or-leave-it way if I would like to come over during the holidays, I didn't find excuses as I might have done a few months earlier but shrugged my shoulders in what I hoped was a gesture every bit as casual as his own, and said: "OK, I might. I'll see what happens."

I let three weeks go by, not to appear eager, and rode out one Saturday midday in a half-empty tram, still sweating and a bit shaky from having committed, on the way, my first desperate act of theft. In my trousers pocket, along with a library card and my tramfare home, were two miniature screwdrivers and a Matchbox jeep, which I would produce dramatically, sometime later that afternoon, as proof positive that I wasn't at all what I seemed, that in spite of my nice accent and the good marks I got at Latin unseens, I was really on the side of disorder and was preparing, behind a show of middle class politeness, to defect.

Johnno met me at the tramstop, wearing an old football jersey that he must have had from primary school and a pair of ragged shorts. I felt overdressed. We walked to his house in sticky silence. He introduced me gruffly to his mother, who looked surprised, as if I wasn't really expected, then positively alarmed when I commented, politely I thought, on her front garden.

"Roses?" she said, as if someone might have smuggled them in when she wasn't looking. "Oh, the roses. Well!"

She stood drying her hands needlessly on a floral apron and Johnno said abruptly, "We're going for a walk." And to me: "Come on, let's piss off."

We went over the sagging fence at the back of his yard and descended through prickly lantana bushes and swathes of orange and yellow nasturtiums into a quarry. It was still and hot. Greenflies clustered on piles of dogshit as we tramped along a festering path and came out into the dazzling arena of the quarry itself. Here, for an hour or so, we made desultory attempts to scale a rockface — Johnno getting higher with his bare feet than I could manage in my best school-shoes — then lay facedown on warm rock and grabbed in the clear-water pools for yabbies, little pale crustaceans that nipped your fingers and when you hauled them out on the sunlit ledge froze into sudden immobility, effacing themselves against the pinkish buff of the stone. We hardly spoke. The two screwdrivers and the Matchbox jeep burned a hole in my pocket but would have to wait. Johnno seemed almost hostile. Why, I wondered, had he bothered to ask me? Why had I come? His attitude to me at school was one of tolerant amusement, which I had come to accept as preferable, at least, to the sort of savagery he reserved for other boys in our class who were equally serious and well-behaved. He never asked to copy my homework. He didn't hustle me into taking bets. He had even joined in once to

41

support me in an argument about the Berlin airlift, then got exasperated and pushed off. This was the first time, I suppose, that we had been alone together for more than five minutes since the old days at Scarborough. Was it because of Scarborough that he made a distinction in my case?

At the far end of the quarry we came to the foot of a long slope that was used by the locals as a tip, and for another half hour I poked about on the edge of it while Johnno waded knee-deep in furry vegetable scraps and climbed high on to a suburban Everest of tin cans, butter boxes, car tyres, enamel basins, old treadle sewing machines, broken venetians, a meatsafe, a punctured waterbag like the one we used to hang on the front of the Hup, dining chairs without seats, paperbacks swollen into a damp wad, and any number of buckled 78's.

"You can find all sorts of things here," Johnno explained unnecessarily. He scrambled down with an old motorbike exhaust. "Can you see anything you want?"

I shrugged my shoulders and looked about in the hope that something small and cleaner than the rest would present itself to my gaze.

"Well, not really," I admitted. My mother would have a fit if I came home with any of this stuff.

"OK then, let's go back."

I had been tempted, while Johnno was scouting about, to make my own contribution to the pile, the screwdrivers etc., which suddenly seemed like an awful mistake, but I was afraid his eagle eye might rediscover them. Instead I hung on, and a little later, in his sleepout room on the side verandah, after we had finished the peanut cookies and milk his mother provided, and listened twice to the Storm from *William Tell*, I produced them, one two three, on the coir mat. Johnno looked puzzled. "I pinched them," I told him hotly, "from Woolworths. On the way through town."

I don't know what I expected exactly. Whatever it was it didn't come. No sign of recognition, no grin of complicity. Instead Johnno looked pained, embarrassed even. His brow puckered. He made a little gesture with his shoulder and turned away to get another record from the pile, and while he cranked furiously at the gramophone handle I sneaked the wretched objects back into my pocket, my face burning with the shame of it all.

For the next half hour we both pretended that nothing had happened, that the two screwdrivers, one red, one green, and the khaki jeep, had never materialized and sat there for a moment on the floor between us. The scratchy gramophone played the Light Cavalry Overture; Toti dal Monte sang "Lo Hear the Gentle Lark"; and a comedian did a piece called "When Father Papered the Parlour", and on the other side "Father O'Flynn". Johnno lounged about flicking through a sports magazine and then fiddled with his crystal set. On the weatherboard wall over his bed were pictures of Don Tallon, a taut blur that was Zatopec winning the fifteen hundred metres, and an old man with a white moustache and a spidery glow around his head who was, Johnno informed me, Albert Schweitzer. When it was time to go he walked me to the tramstop. Or rather, pedalled beside me on his bike, standing high up in the saddle and occasionally making a slow figure-of-eight while I talked my head off. Anything to forget his embarrassment and my own shame.

Because I saw entirely now what it was all about. His embarrassment was for *me*. What I had done was utterly out of character — all I had revealed was my low opinion of *him*. That was what I felt ashamed of now. That I had shown him so openly what I thought of him. He was quieter and more generous than I would have thought possible as I chatted on about the pictures I had seen during the holidays and the girls I had met at Surfers. There was no tram at the terminus, and we waited for what seemed hours before far-off lights appeared in the dusk and the tram could be seen bucketing along through the shopping centre half a mile away, then making its way steeply uphill. Behind us, in the gully, kids were playing on the swings.

Suddenly there was a hissing on the road to our left and a knot of cyclists came flaring into the lighted circle where the tram would turn.

"Hi Johnno. Hi! Hi! Hi!"

They went round again in close formation and came to a halt on the pavement opposite. One of them was Carl Reithmuller. He looked surprised, and a little suspicious I thought, to find me standing with my hands in my pocket at Johnno's tramstop. He looked to Johnno for an explanation.

And if I expected Johnno now to betray whatever loyalty he might have to me and go over to Carl, who stood there gaping expectantly, he surprised me yet again.

"Here's your tram," he said, pushing off into the centre of the road as the tram came sparking around the circle. "I'll see you."

Carl looked confused.

"What we doing then, Johnno? Where're we going?" He pushed off. And the others set themselves in motion behind him, wheeling about on the road like big heavy birds, making uneasy shadows in the dusk.

"Go where you like," Johnno told him sharply, "I'm off home", and he sped away downhill leaving the others to regroup, turn, and hiss off after him.

I climbed into the compartment at the back of the tram and waited, while the driver and the conductor sat with their feet up blowing smoke across the car. I felt miserable. Taking the two screwdrivers out of my pocket I placed them carefully on the seat between me and the wall, then added, furtively, the model jeep. And there I would leave them, by accident as it were, when I pulled the bell and got off.

IV

Johnno didn't fail the Junior after all. He even did well. And when the school year began he appeared before us in an utterly new light: the flamboyant waves had given way to a neat brushback; he had no further interest in the SP business, though he still spent long hours studying the racing forms; he even turned, suddenly, into a sporting type, and could be seen most dinner-hours in singlet and spiked shoes jogging round the sodden oval, or doing press-ups on the grass.

"He's putting it on," people told one another, hoping it was true. "It's a swindle. You'll see."

But the weeks went by, and except for rare flashes the old Johnno failed to reappear. He did his own homework, kept his own notes, and was generally considered nobody's fool. In the early days, when he got up and asked one of his involved questions, we were inclined to giggle, expecting some sort of elaborate joke. But even masters had to admit at last that he was a reformed character. "It's unbelievable," people said, finding it just a little dishonest of him to have been, all this time, something other than a buffoon. Even Soapy had to accept, reluctantly, that Johnno's interest in geology was genuine after all and that he was making fair to be his star pupil. He looked grumpy and out of sorts.

46

One factor in Johnno's transformation was the absence of what we had called The Boys. Stal Henderson had gone onto his father's property. "I don't care," he had boasted once when Soapy warned him he would never get the Junior, "I'm going on the land." And Soapy: "What as, boy, manure?" Carl Reithmuller was at Dalgetys, the Mango was a storeman at Edwards and Lambs. Free at last of their expectations, Johnno had simply settled and become himself.

Or had he? Was there really a change? We watched him closely, waiting for the new Johnno to crack, waiting for him to give up this silly pretence that he wasn't what we had long since accepted him as, our very own Tamburlaine and Al Capone, the one among us who could be depended upon to reject everything that was decent, respectable, sensible even, and take off on his own extravagant parabola, that would lead who-knows-where? Was he about to settle, after all, for the *predictable*? We simply refused to believe it, and he was forever being called upon to repeat some old triumph from his repertoire of burps and farts, or to live over again some piece of outrageous buffoonery that had become part of the Johnno legend. On such occasions he would redden and look pained. It was, I suppose, a kind of meanness in us to insist that the old Johnno should not die, and I thought hotly of my screwdrivers. If Johnno was not Johnno where did any of us stand? But changes can't be resisted, and we might have observed, if we had bothered to look, that he had ceased to be an ugly duckling, all arms and legs, with a head too big for his body, and had developed, as if to match his aspirations, the long hard lines of an athlete. He was tall, well-knit, relaxed as he jogged round the oval in his spiked shoes; and girls, if they hadn't been scared off by the tales they had heard of him, might even have found him good looking. He had simply outgrown our idea of him, and we found it difficult to accept the fact without making allowance for commensurate changes in ourselves.

I was utterly bewildered. Ever since those days, long ago at Scarborough, when Johnno had been identified for me as "bad company", I had used him as a marker. His wildness had been a powerful warning to me in those carrot-chewing days when I thought bad habits meant not getting your homework done as soon as you got in from school, and lately it had come to seem a marvellously liberating alternative to my own wishy-washy and hypocritical niceness. Now all that was changed. I didn't know where I was. What made me most resentful, I think, was his refusal to stay still. I had found for Johnno a place in what I thought of as *my* world and he refused to stay there or to play the minor role I had assigned him. He had suddenly developed qualities of his own, complexities I hadn't allowed for. I had to admit with something like panic that he might even be as sensitive, in his own way, as myself! I began to wonder if Johnno's old daring hadn't been an atonement for *our* cowardice; an attempt to shame us out of timidity. Everything I had ever seen of him in these last years began to shift and change its ground. Maybe, after all, it was Johnno who was the deep one.

I was surprised, given what had happened over the holidays, that he showed so little animosity towards me. We didn't become friends exactly, but there was

48

an understanding between us just the same. It was sporadic, unstated, but it existed, and came out in his occasional teasing of me. Once, years ago, he had called me "The Prof". Now, after the appearance in the school magazine of a poem "To Beatrice" (its real subject, in fact, was a sleepy, chestnut-headed sixth-former), he dubbed me "Dante". I hated it but the name stuck. At the very moment when I was most in doubt about who I was, or where I stood, I had developed a new identity and now not even the name sewn into my gym things was true . . .

Arran Avenue, Hamilton, Brisbane, Queensland, Australia, the World. That is the address that appears in my schoolbooks. But what does it mean? Where do I really stand?

The house at Arran Avenue is the grim, three-storeyed brick house my father built for us in one of the best suburbs in Brisbane. Arran Avenue is a narrow dead-end street that runs straight into the hillside, with houses piled steeply one above the other on either side and bush beginning where the bitumen peters out into a track. The traffic of Kingsford Smith Drive is less than fifty yards away but cannot be heard. The river, visible from the terrace outside my parents' bedroom, widens here to a broad stream, low mudflats on one bank, with a colony of pelicans, and on the other steep hills covered with native pine, across which the switchback streets climb between gullies of morning glory and high creeper-covered walls.

It is a house I have never got used to. Waking sometimes in the night I am still momentarily alarmed to find that I am not back in my bedroom at Edmondstone Street, listening to the shunting and clashing of trains at Kyogle Station and watching the shadow of staghorns and ferns on the wax-papered window. Arran Avenue Hamilton, as an address, seems slightly false. My loyalties remain where my feelings are, at the old house, with the corrugated-iron fence at the bottom of the yard leaning uneasily into the next street, and Musgrave Park with its insect-swarming darkness under the Moreton Bay figs still crowded with metho drinkers — disreputable, certainly, but warmer, more mysterious than Arran Avenue Hamilton, where everything is glossy and modern: electric stove, washing machine, built-in cupboards instead of the old pantry, a tiled niche for the refrigerator.

I sit in my room at the back of the house and let my mind drift away from Cicero's *Pro Ligario* or a problem in perms and coms. Outside little treefrogs are clinking away under a wall — clink, clink, the sound that stars might make. Behind me my parents are sitting up in bed reading the *Telegraph*, which is full of aggravated assaults and traffic offences, sipping tea which my father makes from his "galley" at the top of the stairs, listening to an all-night radio station. What do I have to do with all this, I wonder? I feel odd and independent. There is nothing in what I think or feel these days that relates to my parents, to what they know or might have taught me, nothing at all. Or so I believe. I have left their influence far behind me: having learned at last to drink beer (though my father is a fanatical teetotaller), and to have left-wing opinions and despise the world of business. We have nothing in common now. Sometimes, seeing a light under the door, my father will step in and say: "I think you'd better get to bed son. You don't want to read *too* much." He picks up one of my books and weighs it on the palm of his hand. What he means is that books are useless (certainly he's never found any use for them) and might even be a bit effeminate. He distrusts their influence on me. In weighing them on his palm like that he is testing the enemy. Proud as he is of any success I might have at school, he would prefer me to get out into the world and start on my own account, as he did, instead of experiencing everything second hand, through books. This is a matter on which he and my mother disagree. She would like me to be a doctor, or to go in for the law. How little they understand me! What I am, what I will be, can have nothing to do with them. I feel like a stranger in the house. And what irritates me most of all, is that there is absolutely no hostility between us — they are ideal parents, I have nothing to complain of, they leave me no room to rebel.

As for Brisbane, the city I have been born in — well, what can anyone say about *that*? I have been reading Dante. His love for *his* city is immense, it fills his whole life, its streets, its gardens, its people; it is a force that has shaped his whole being. Have I been shaped in any way — fearful prospect! — by Brisbane? Our big country town that is still mostly weather-board and one-storeyed, so little a city that on Friday morning the C.W.A. ladies set their stalls up in Queen Street and sell home-made cakes and jam, and the farmers come in with day-old chicks in wire baskets. Brisbane is so sleepy, so slatternly, so sprawlingly un-lovely! I have taken to wandering about after school

51

looking for one simple object in it that might be romantic, or appalling even, but there is nothing. It is simply the most ordinary place in the world.

Arran Avenue, Hamilton, Brisbane, Queensland . . .

Queensland, of course, is a joke. The Moonshine State. Nothing to be said about Queensland. Half of it is still wild (there are tigers as yet undiscovered in Cape York Peninsula according to some authorities), the rest detained in a sort of perpetual nineteenth century. In the main streets of towns not a hundred miles from where I am sitting they still have hitching-posts. Aborigines are herded on to reservations. Kids, even in this well-to-do suburb, go to school all the year round with bare feet.

What an extraordinary thing it is, that I should be here rather than somewhere else. If my father's father hadn't packed up one day to escape military service under the Turks; if my mother's people, for God knows what reason, hadn't decided to leave their comfortable middle class house at New Cross for the goldfields of Mount Morgan, I wouldn't be an Australian at all. It is practically an accident, an entirely unnecessary fate.

Arran Avenue, Hamilton, Brisbane, Australia . . . Why Australia? What *is* Australia anyway?

The continent itself is clear enough, burned into my mind on long hot afternoons in Third Grade, when I learned to sketch in its irregular coastline: the half-circle of the Great Australian Bight, the little booted foot of Eyre's Peninsula, Spencer's Gulf down to Port Phillip, up the easy east coast, with its slight belly at Brisbane, towards Sandy Cape and Cape York; round the Gulf of Carpentaria and

Arnhem Land to the difficulties of King Sound and the scoop towards North West Cape where I always go wrong, leaving the spurred heel of Cape Leeuwin so far out in the Indian Ocean that it would wreck every liner afloat, or so close in to the Bight that far-off Western Australia looks as if it's been stricken with polio. I know the outline; I know the names (learned painfully for homework) of several dozen capes, bays, promontories; and can trace in with a dotted line the hopeless journeys across it of all the great explorers, Sturt, Leichhardt, Burke and Wills. But what it is beyond that is a mystery. It is what begins with the darkness at our back door. Too big to hold in the mind! I think my way out a few steps into it and give up on the slopes of a Mount Hopeless that is just over the fence in the vacant allotment next door. Australia is impossible! Hardly worth thinking about.

And the World?

The World, as the headmaster tells us severely at his weekly "peptalks", is what we are about to be tested against. He has recently come to us from the Royal Military College at Duntroon and is much impressed with the amount of gold lettering on our honour-boards — a whole generation lost but not forgotten: *Baptism of Fire, Glory of Young Manhood, Corner of a Forgotten Field*. The Korean War has recently burst upon us and shows no sign of abating before we will be old enough to go. The headmaster regards us tragically and sticks out his shaven jaw: *Spirit of Anzac still alive among us, Everlasting Flame, Fine Old Tradition, Challenge of Battle — Not Forgetting the Wives and Mothers. Out into Life with Courage and a Firm Tread*, in two lines, and *without* talking . . .

Meanwhile, we prepared:

Moss's Dancing Academy was a gloomy, refined establishment in the basement of an insurance building, where boys and girls of the better schools (non-Catholic) learned dancing, made innocent or not so innocent assignations, and planned the week's social round of barbecues, coming-out dances, end-of-term hops, tennis parties, swimming parties, picnics, and Sunday excursions to the coast. Moss's was eminently respectable and stiflingly genteel. We learned the quickstep, the jazz waltz, the Pride of Erin, the Gipsy Tap — and as a gesture towards the late forties, the Samba, whose respectability was guaranteed by its being the favourite modern dance of Princess Margaret. Tall, blank-faced, utterly unsexy, Mr. Moss's "ladies" were to be seen each week pushing new boys a good head shorter than themselves round the boraxed floor while Victor Silvester oozed sweetly from a radiogram. Those of us who had graduated danced with *real* girls (Test of Manhood) who sat in rows along the wall opposite and waited demurely to be asked. At a clap of Mr. Moss's plump, hairy hands, we crossed the floor in a mob, some of us actually *sliding*, and did not actually grab the girls, which was barbarous ("Barbarous" Mr. Moss would shout above the melee), but surged and jostled around the most popular of them, insisting breathlessly: "Excuse me — I was here first! — could I have the pleasure? — get lost! — would you care to dance?" If the young lady said: "No thank you, I

54

think I'll sit this one out", you asked someone else (never of course anyone close enough to see that she hadn't been your first choice), or slouched off crest-fallen to the boys' side of the room, where a group of the shy, the rejected, the frankly uninterested would be gathered around the Coke-box, engaged in a noisy argument about motorbikes or the selection of a team.

Johnno was a conspicuous figure at Moss's, lounging against a pillar in what was considered to be a bold manner as he eyed up the prospects, or coltishly jerking at his collar while he prepared to join the rush. He was known to be experienced, and this gave him an aura of dangerous charm. Girls flustered at his approach. He had been on weekends to the Coast, only sixty miles from staid, old-fashioned Brisbane, but already in those days the centre of a wickedly alternative life. Among its harlequin motels, Florida, El Dorado, Las Vegas, call-girls had begun to operate, and a fast crowd from the South was continuously at play. Johnno brought back fabulous tales of his exploits among the wives of Melbourne bookmakers and nurses up in groups for the winter. He had spent a whole weekend once with a tart and her protector who were travelling round Australia in a caravan. Two queers had offered to take him to Hong Kong. When pressed for details Johnno shrugged, looked in-scrutable, then gave one of his big, open grins. Were his stories true? Who could tell? They were probable enough, given Johnno, given the place. He had even been, it seems, to one of the brothels in Albert Street, which we had all driven past at one time or another, hoping for an eyeful of one of the girls in high-heeled shoes and evening dress tucked up in front like Betty

Grable; but Johnno had actually been in. The corrugated-iron wall, with its little gate, exerted a fascination over us that Johnno's shrugs, his looks of bored insouciance, did nothing to dispel. Lolling against a pillar on the boys' side of the room, or against the verandah rails at a Boatshed dance, Johnno was devastatingly cool and in control. Almost, in fact, a "golden boy". And one of the things we now had to admit about him was that this too was one of the possibilities that had brushed his shoulder and was waiting invitingly to be taken up, the possibility of his joining the little group of the elect among us, the handsome, the athletic, the socially assured, who had been marked out for *success*. But, for some reason, it was a possibility he had already determined to reject. His parody of the Golden Boys was relentless. He hated them with a deadly hatred that could only have its origin, I decided, in something he had discovered in himself. Faced with their clean lines, their glowing good health, their poise, he turned surly; he slouched, he jerked at his collar, he moved his shoulders about, gangster-fashion, under their pads, he was brutally frank. "I'm just here for the sex," he'd announce to the stiff-shirted, black-tie brigade, "what are you here for?" Or at Moss's dreamily, through ground teeth: "Jesus! Just look at those tits!" But in mixed company, I noticed, some of his coolness deserted him. He looked oddly ill-at-ease. He didn't know what to do with his hands.

Test of Manhood . . .

I had fallen heavily in my last year for a Somerville House girl called Roseanne Staples, who wore nylon stockings that shifted their lights like mother of pearl and was a G.P.S. diving champion. All one Wednesday

56

at Moss's, and again the next, we danced dreamily under the rafters and I took her afterwards for mint juleps or malteds at the Pig 'n Whistle, a milk bar at the top of town that had been a favourite pick-up place for American soldiers and retained something of its wartime glamour and notoriety. It was regarded as daring and I was out to impress. When the waitress, who looked as if she might remember the place in the old days, slid our milk-shakes down the glass-topped counter, she winked in the direction of the innocent Roseanne and whispered: "There y'are love. That'll put lead in yer pencil." I could hardly wait for the week to pass. But on the third Wednesday, as we went whirling across the floor in what seemed to be a most accomplished manner, Roseanne, with a casualness that astonishes me even today, it was so low-keyed, so undramatic, pronounced the words that put an end to our affair, pfft! just like that, and changed the course of my life. Looking straight over my shoulder, in the most neutral tones: "If there's one thing I can't stand," said Roseanne Staples, slowly, "it's boys who don't pivot."

I was thunderstruck. The pivot — that little side-step and pass at the corner of the floor that I had never quite got the knack of, it seemed so silly, hardly worth worrying about. I smiled wanly and guided her through the rest of the set, closing my eyes and swallowing hard as we approached the corners and wishing Moss's was triangular. *Four* corners was suddenly more than I could bear. Back safe among the boys I waited for something less subtle, like a Gipsy Tap.

So much then for the test of manhood. There were things they hadn't warned us of, pitfalls in the

57

corners of rooms, girls who would expect you to pivot and perform God knows what prodigies. There was also the Cold War, the Cobalt Bomb, pre-marital intercourse, the death of God — it was a battlefield, as the headmaster had warned us, and I thought with envy of all those old boys whose names were picked out in gold on the honour-boards, lying safe in some corner of a foreign field that would be forever Wynnum or Coorparoo. Ours was to be a quiet generation. It was the little tests that would break us (not forgetting the wives and mothers) and there was no one to help us through.

V

I saw very little of Johnno in our first months at university. He was reading geology, and we had no occasion to meet except briefly in one of the crowded refectories, or on one of the even more crowded buses. Later I began to run into him at the Public Library, where he was regularly installed behind a tower of books in one of the corners under the stairs; but the library wasn't a place where you could talk. He would give me a wink, or nod uncommittally as I turned past him up one of the iron stairways, and sometimes I would catch him looking up through the railings of the gallery to where I sat chewing the end of a pencil or staring out across the muddy river. We seldom did more than pass the time of day. On one occasion I remember he came to where I was sitting and pushed a book across the table. "Here," he said gruffly, "see what you think of this", then slouched off. It was *The Birth of Tragedy*. I saw him again a week or so later, and after a good deal of hesitation, went across. "I read the book," I told him. In fact it had excited me enormously, and I had thought, reading between the lines, that I could see why he had given it to me, what it was he wanted me to see. Now he looked up vaguely, and blinked his china-blue eyes. "Oh?" When I began to tell him how much I was interested by it he looked put out, cut me off short, and damn him! I thought, drifting back to my place. But he was always there, large and hunch-shouldered in his niche under the stairs, and I knew that we would eventually come together, though neither of us was in a hurry about it.

The Public Library in those days was its own strange hermetic world. I could have written an anthropological study of its inhabitants, I spent so much time there (and so much of it staring up from my Latin proses), or an ecological treatise on the peppery dust that itched in your nostrils, and the colourless mites that crawled out of its woodwork and tumbled from the pages of its crumbly books; or provided a guidebook to the corners, behind a stair-case or in the bays of its upper galleries, that were all but invisible, and the places from which a view could be had of everyone who came and went in the hall. In winter, draughts got in under the floorboards, and the dingy brown linoleum lifted under your feet, it was like walking on the muddy waves of the river whose mangroves and sluggish grey-brown waters lapped beyond the sill. On real scorchers in summer the heat would set off an alarm at the local fire station, and a dozen burly firemen, with asbestos suits and burnished helmets, would burst into the silence, stand about looking foolish for a while in sweaty clumps, then creep off down the stairs.

The library had its own people. You never saw them anywhere else in the city, except there, or on the buttoned-leather couches at the School of Arts: old men with watery red-rimmed eyes and no collar to their shirt, who settled somewhere as soon as the library opened at ten in the morning and stayed put till it was time to queue at the Salvation Army

Refuge or the St. Vincent de Paul, about an hour before dusk. They slept mostly, and had to be prodded when they snored. One or two of them were such powerful presences that they belonged to the place as completely, almost, as the Chief Librarian himself. They had their own tables, received visitors there, and their name, and some version of their story, was known to every one of us.

There was Old Moscow for instance. He was a White Russian, and was supposed to have been Professor of Law at Moscow University — before the revolution, of course. A huge man, amiable, inarticulate, with a flat face and wiry grey hairs sprouting above his flannel vest, he sat in state at the very centre of the hall and no one ever disturbed him. Sometimes a new librarian, hoping to make an impression and ignorant of the traditions of the place, would decide to move him on or to keep him quiet, and there would be a noisy affray. Moscow was immovable. And the poor girl, repenting of her officiousness, would soon be as fond of him — as frightened of him — as the rest. When aroused he had a big booming voice that filled the whole building from floor to iron ceiling, and the flow of his Russian (if that is what it was) was terrifying. But left to his own devices he was entirely harmless. He occupied his table at the centre and beamed upon us, as if we were all somehow under his watchful but benign scrutiny. I thought of some senior officer of the Russian Civil Service (I had been reading Gogol), complacently dreaming of birch forests and dead souls while we slaved over our ninety-seven cases of Constitutional Law.

Old Moscow and the other vagrant people haunted

61

me, I was fascinated by them. They shuffled into the library from nowhere. From the Domain, with its cluster of broken-down army huts; from Musgrave Park where I had watched them as a child, in pools of darkness under the Moreton Bay figs; from Albert Park above Roma Street Station and the arcades of the old markets in Turbot Street, where they were still to be seen sometimes, in the early morning, wrapped up in newspapers like old parcels, or in dirty vegetable sacks. And when the rest of us were packing up at nightfall to go home to our warm roast dinners, they went back again. To nowhere. To sleep in suburban tramsheds and ferry shelters, or on the waste ground under Grey Street Bridge.

How, I wondered, had they fallen out of that safe and regular world that the rest of us took for granted as if it was the only world there could be? Success wasn't inevitable after all. Sitting among us, as we struggled with Kant's categorical imperative and the Elizabethan love lyric, were some who had already been chosen, perhaps, to be the failures, and might have seen in Old Moscow and the rest, if they had had the eyes of prophecy, their own terrible old age in this slatternly town, sleeping in gutters outside the Valley wine bars, following Abo women up Fish Lane near the bridge, beating someone to death in the marshes along Victoria Park golf-links for half a bottle of metho. Life suddenly seemed utterly mysterious to me. What were the mechanics of survival? What did you have to do to stay afloat?

VI

Johnno and I did have our meeting at last, one cold dry night in July, as I was on my way home from a lecture.

A westerly was blowing. It came straight in off the river, and the few late travellers like myself battled across the open space in front of the Treasury, heads down, coats flapping, and disappeared into doorways along the Quay to be out of it. The shadow of palm trees flared on the pavement as the big overhead lamps swung and rattled. Brisbane westerlies have an edge of ice to them. The shaggy frost of Stanthorpe orchards and the cold of miles on miles of open Downs comes hurling in through the Gap, and makes vicious eddies at every street corner, a whirlwind of little sharp grits. Even here, deep in the entrance to a fruitshop, the wind still cut my face and smarted in my eyes. Slipping out again, I got round the corner into George Street. I wouldn't be able to see my tram from here, but if I stood close to the pavement and kept my ears cocked I would hear the clash of the sparking-pole as it rattled in across the bridge.

Suddenly I was aware of a slithering in the darkness behind me. Someone was down there on the floor, against the door to the shop. A wino, or a metho-drinker. I prepared to dive out again into the shop next door.

"Hullo Dante," a voice said, as the green neon opposite washed in over us.

I recognized him immediately. He was sprawled out on the dirty floor, his hair a birds' nest. Grinning.

"It's all right," he said, reassuringly. "I'm only drunk. Haven't you seen anyone pissed before? No, no — don't bother. I can manage."

He struggled upright in the darkness, and when the green light flooded into the deep entrance again he was half-standing against the door.

"See?"

The light drained out, and in the darkness I heard him slip. Cursing.

"As a matter of fac', Dante," he admitted, "I do need a bit of a hand. I just haven't got a clue where I bloody *am*."

I got him up off the floor (he made heavy weather of it — deliberately, I thought) and out into the street.

"Really Dante, this is bloody good of you. It is! I want to be frank with you, I've been drinking. In fac', I am absolutely — bloody — PISSED."

I took his arm. "You told me that before."

"Oh, did I? Well it's th' truth. I'm pissed as a newt!"

Ten minutes later, sitting opposite in the cabin of a tram, he regarded me with serious amusement. He had seemed so drunk at the tramstop that I'd decided to take him home. Now, mysteriously, he was almost sober. The tram was empty and it travelled fast. Shut up in the lighted cabin it was like flying through the dark; the tram bucked and swayed, the street lamps dipped away downhill, a line of palms on Red Hill tossed wildly against ragged cloud that streamed away faster even than ourselves, flickering across the face of the moon. Even if we had wanted to, what with the wheels clashing underneath and the rush of air, we couldn't have heard each other speak.

We rode all the way to the terminus. I knew the way from there, and had no trouble till we reached the lawn of his house, which was in a gully out of the wind. A plaster heron stood on one leg in front of an empty bird-bath, and there were two frogs on the grass, one as big as a spaniel.

"Pets," Johnno explained, squatting on the lawn between them. "China ones, that don't do you-know-what." He grinned up at me, then stretched out full length with his arms folded on his chest and the big frog at his feet.

"Dead."

"I'd better be going," I told him shortly. I had been led a good hour out of my way and was fed up with him.

He sat up. "Well just ring that bell first, will you?" He directed me in the dark. "Beside the lattice. No, no — on the left. That's it." A light bloomed in the depths of the house and the lattice fell in shadow across the lawn. Johnno's mother on the other side peered at me apprehensively.

"It's alright," Johnno called, "I'm pissed again and someone's brought me home. You remember Dante. He's coming in for some coffee."

Inside he flopped full length into one of the genoa-velvet armchairs and closed his eyes. His mother, in a knitted cardigan that might have been his father's, stood with her arms folded and regarded him.

"Don't you take any notice of him," she told me, "he's got no manners. No sense either!" She gave him a sharp kick with her woolly slipper and Johnno opened one eye and swore. "Do you have your coffee made of milk, or black like him?"

"Black," I admitted.

"See!" Johnno said, and she turned on her heel and disappeared. Almost immediately there was the sound of drumming water and the hiss of gas. I let my eye travel round the room: yellowing silk lampshade with tassels; strings of beads in the doorway leading to the verandah; some lumpish examples of night-school pottery. Sunk between the arms of his chair Johnno followed my gaze.

"Hideous, isn't it?"

The coffee arrived.

"And don't knock it over," she told him as she set the tray down at his elbow, "it's just behind you." Johnno hauled himself up and sipped his coffee noisily.

"I've just finished that book," she announced.

Johnno grunted.

She turned to me.

"Do you know Voltaire?" she enquired, poised on the very edge of her seat and ready for conversation.

"Oh Jesus," Johnno exploded. "Why do you jump on people the moment they get into the house?"

She made a prim line with her lips. Ignoring him. "He's drunk," she said, "take no notice of him. You'd think he'd be pleased I'm not one of these silly women who are out playing bridge all day and read nothing but the *Women's Weekly*. In fact *he's* the one who gave me Voltaire. Yes you did! Now he's mad because I've actually read it. We can ignore him, he's not in a fit state."

I made a feeble attempt to formulate some

thoughts on *Candide* — the earthquake at Lisbon — and Johnno groaned.

"You see," he told her fiercely, "he's embarrassed. You embarrass people."

"I do not. You're the one who embarrasses them. Have I embarrassed you?" she demanded. "Have I?"

"Well go on Dante. Are you embarrassed?" Johnno was enjoying himself now. "Of course he's embarrassed!"

She turned her back on him. "Do go on Dante, that was very interesting," she told me sweetly. "He can't discuss anything in a normal, civilized way."

"That," Johnno said, "is because you haven't the smallest understanding of anything you read."

"I do so too."

"You don't. It might just as well be the *Women's Weekly*."

"You're drunk," she said. And to me: "He's just being difficult. Go to bed," she snapped, "if you can't be decent."

"Poor Dante, he's so embarrassed," Johnno said again. "Can't you see that? He's not used to it. Not everyone carries on the way you do."

"The way *you* do, you mean."

They both looked at me.

"You must come again," Johnno's mother insisted at the verandah. "Come and have tea. It's a pleasure to meet someone *sober* for a change. Instead of his usual rowdies."

"G'night, Dante," Johnno called from the depths of his chair.

One Friday night, two or three weeks later, there

was a telephone call.

"Hullo, hullo. Is this Dante?"

The voice sounded far off as if it might be a trunk call from overseas. There was a lot of crackling and a roar like ocean waves crashing and sucking away.

"This is Johnno."

I put my hand over the receiver and told my sister, who had come to the top of the stairs and was listening, to go away.

"Hullo. Hullo! Dante! Are you still there?"

"Yes, I'm here. I was just talking to someone."

"Oh, I thought we'd been cut off." There was silence filled with the same hissing and crackling as before. Rain seeping into the cables perhaps. "Look, I'm in town. Could you come in and meet me?"

"Now?"

"Of course now!"

"Well — what time is it?"

"Oh Jesus. I don't know what time it is. What do you want to know the time for? About half-past nine I think. The point is, will you come?"

"Well, I — "

"Alright then, forget it!"

"No, no. listen — "

I extended the phone to the length of its cord and leaned back to see the time on our hall clock. It was twenty past nine. What excuse could I possibly give for getting dressed at this hour and going all the way into town? In the dead of night, my mother would call it.

"Listen, Johnno. I mean, is it important?"

"Of course it's important. Why can't you ever do anything without asking questions? I'm pissed as a matter of fact. I need to sit down somewhere and sober up. I need someone to talk to. Otherwise I'll just fall down in the rain and the coppers'll get me . . . "

"Where are you then?"

"Post Office. Can't you hear the wind? Here, have a listen." And he must have held the receiver out of the half-cabinet because the swirling sound filled my ears again. It was a westerly howling through the post office arcade.

"OK then. Where will I find you?"

"Criterion. You know where it is?"

"Of course I do."

"Well, then. George Street entrance. I'll be on the right as you come in."

I was about to put the receiver down when he was suddenly calling again from the other end of the line.

"Listen," he said. "Do you know this?"

He began to whistle, twenty bars of something shrill and tuneless that I could make no sense of. The notes, coming and going on the sea sounds as the wind sucked and sighed, were indescribably eerie. There were gaps as he paused to take breath.

"Well," he asked, "did you recognize it?"

I had to admit I didn't.

"Oh." He sounded disappointed. "I thought you might know it. It's Mozart's something or other. Well never mind. I'll see you in half an hour."

After that he rang regularly, and we began to spend Friday nights together in one of the three or four city pubs where they never asked your age. One of them was always the Criterion. Others were the Lands

Office in George Street, the Prince Consort in the Valley, a big old-fashioned pub with two cast-iron balconies, and best of all, the Grand Central.

The Grand Central had been the scene during the war of a famous brawl, when Australian and American servicemen had fought the whole of one Saturday night all up and down the inner city. In the morning there were seven dead. Or three. Or five. It was an important episode in Brisbane's wartime legend. Now the Grand Central was the drinking place of "Nashos"; it had a queer bar, a plush and cut-glass ladies lounge on the second floor, and at the very back (with its own entrance in the street behind) an open air beer garden, all green-stained concrete and wrought-iron tables, that was known as the Sex Pit, since it was the special preserve of Brisbane's most flamboyant tarts. They occupied a table apiece, wore glossy patent-leather shoes, carried glossy patent-leather handbags, had their hair lacquered and piled up in sculptured jet-black, peroxide, or chestnut curls, pencilled eyebrows, vivid scarlet mouths — they were the real thing. Potted palms gave the Sex Pit an air of the jungle. The pavement was creviced and discoloured, and occasionally a big elephant beetle with curved horns emerged from one of the cracks and caused consternation as it waddled across the floor or barged about in the heavy air.

"Just look at them," Johnno would hiss delightedly, "the whores."

They sat with their legs crossed, looking bored, and one of them might take an emery stick from her handbag, snapping it shut with an audible click, and saw away at her nails.

"Aren't they marvellous!"

70

It was, I think, their theatricality that appealed to him, the high gloss of their finish, their perfect approximation to the idea of "whore" that he had derived from his reading. We struck up an acquaintance with one or two of them and got to know their names.

"DULcie," Johnno would intone in a sort of rapturous daze. "Le-ON-a. VAL-may. Dor-EEN."

But mostly we were too late for the Grand Central.

I had started going to the Stadium on Friday nights with my father. He had always wanted me to be an athlete of some sort. Years ago, when I was a small boy, he had taken me to see an old boxing mate who was attempting a ball-punching record, and I had watched fascinated and horrified while the man, half-dead on his feet, jabbed doggedly at the ball, hissing weakly through his nostrils, then collapsed at the hour break into the arms of his supporters, his whole body shaken and streaming with sweat. For my next birthday I had a pair of boxing gloves, but every effort to teach me to hiss through my nose and jab and poke and put up a guard proved hopeless. I didn't have the spirit for it. One whole summer when I was ten he had me get up at five-thirty and stroke up and down the Valley pool, while he timed me with a stop-watch, and when winter came and the pool was closed I performed exercises with a machine he had rigged up in our spare room, a plank with weights on leather straps that I hauled at for ten minutes at a time. But that was the end of it. No more! I refused absolutely to have anything to do with it: swimming, boxing, football, the lot. It was a terrible disappointment to him. Now, at twenty, I felt some need to make reparations. We went together to the

Fights, sitting high up in the "bleachers", and my father began to teach me the fine points of the game.

He had an eye for the "particular fault" in a boxer that made every fight for him an Aristotelian tragedy, though he would never have recognized it as such.

"The left," he would say, sadly, the moment a boxer shaped up. Or "Watch the belly" — And sure enough, later, the tough self-confident boy in black shorts who had come bouncing into the ring and done his little dance of triumph for the crowd, a clear winner, would be spread-eagled on the canvas while the referee counted over him, *eight, nine*, and the crowd rose to its feet in the smoky hall, shouting, whistling, banging on their stalls.

I hated the Fights and couldn't leave them alone. They had a brutal simplicity. There was always a winner; there was always somebody, hunch-shouldered, dancing out bloody-nosed to shake hands, whose final weakness had been exposed to us all — the loser. And there was always a reason why he lost. "The left," my father would murmur. He could see it all from the beginning. The fight itself was a ritual in which the loser fought heroically against his own weakness, against a fate that was already decided, and to the expert, visible from the start: a weak limb, bad training, too much grog, too many women, or the sheer arrogance and folly of not knowing your own limits. "He's a good lad," my father would say as the trainer cuffed the ear of a loser. "He put up a good show." It was the losers he kept his eye on. The quick, sure-footed champions bored him, he could see their qualities too clearly. There was nothing at stake as they backed off hissing and waited on springy tiptoe to be allowed in for the kill. That is, till they too started downhill: slowed up, put on weight, got careless, over-confident.

He knew what it was to be a winner. He had never lost a fight himself, except to a real champ, Archie Bradley, and had retired without a scar. What it was to be a loser was something else again . . .

When the Fights were over Johnno would be waiting and we would set off on our tramp round the town.

"Look after yourself, son" was all my father would offer in the way of advice. He had come up the hard way, learning to scrap in the "pushes" that terrorized the Southside before the Great War, and at the same time going to mass every morning and after work making deliveries with his horse and sulky for the St. Vincent de Paul. He was a mixture of knockabout worldliness and the most extraordinary innocence. I have no idea what he thought we were doing in that disreputable part of Brisbane so late at night, or if he thought anything at all. He never asked questions, he never gave the smallest hint that he was aware of what was going on about him. There was a hot-dog man at the door of the bleachers. "If you've been t' the fight and yer going t' fuck, y' need a hot dog" he would bellow as the crowd streamed out and made its way towards the darkened streets between the Stadium and the Gardens. My father never raised an eyebrow.

VII

I don't know when Johnno discovered the Greek
Club, or how, but that was where we were to be
found most often on those Friday nights, and the
long dimly lighted room, with its marble-topped bar
and tables, its blacked out windows and sawdust
floor, is irrevocably associated in my mind with his
conspiratorial phase.

The barman, a sleepy, bare-armed Cretan called
Stavros, served us cognac with little sideplates of
tomato and olives. From the next room came the
pock of billiard balls, and an occasional cry from half
a dozen throats as a spectacular win was made at one
of the card tables, where dark, moustachioed figures
sat close under the lamps in a fog of driftless smoke.
Sometime towards midnight a boy would appear,
sprinkle the sawdust from a watering can, and sweep
it up, greyish and foul with butts. Stavros would sleep
with his thick head on his arm, till he was called from
the doorway for another round of drinks and sideplates of fetta and olives. Or he would walk to the
doorway and stand with his hands on his hips in the
smoky lightshaft, while some tense moment passed in
the play, shaking his head and shrugging his shoulders
at us as he passed — someone had just lost a small
fortune in there! And Johnno, responsive to the

74

atmosphere of the place, and to the effects of the raw cognac, would begin hinting at some new revelation that he was about to make, lowering his voice across the table to the merest whisper. Though there was no one but Stavros to hear us. And he knew no English.

"It's something I heard last year," he would whisper, "when I was on mining practice at Rosebery. From this Pole. Well, he was a count actually, but of course he doesn't use his title out here. We called him Mike."

He would take another sip of his cognac and lean closer.

"Only you've got to swear you won't tell, Dante. I'm not joking, you've really got to swear and mean it. A man's life could be at stake."

I look sceptical. I've heard all this before.

"Will you swear then? It's for your own sake as much as anyone else's. They'd be after you like a shot if they thought you knew."

"Who would?"

Johnno leans back and smiles.

"Ah — well that's just the point, isn't it? That's what I'm going to tell you. Only you've got to swear."

I do so, with a reserve of irony that Johnno pretends not to notice, raising my right hand Scout-fashion and repeating an oath. Johnno isn't exactly pleased but it will do.

"Well then," he whispers, "it's the Organization, see? The big one, the one that's behind everything, wars, revolutions, depressions, the lot. We think they just happen. Twenty-four causes of the French Revolution and all that bullshit. Trade barriers, currency restrictions, economics. Human nature! And all the time it's *them*. They're sitting round a table somewhere, or contacting one another by secret radio. Boom! There's a palace revolution in Jordan, someone's knocked off quietly in Colombia, the drachma collapses. A plane crash. A world war. It's them every time."

Johnno sits back, sips at his drink, considers the effect upon me of this shattering revelation. I shrug my shoulders. He crouches towards me. "And who do you think they are," he asks darkly. "Can you guess?"

I have recently been developing a taste for irony.

"World Jewry?" I hazard. "The Church?"

The effect on Johnno quite alarms me. He jerks forward, shoots me a glance that is full of suspicion, recovers, watches me closely as he drains his glass.

"As a matter of fact, Dante, you're closer than you think." His voice becomes almost inaudible. "World Jewry, the Church, the Masons — all three of them working together! Isn't that something? Think of all those poor fools who think the Catholics and the Masons are sworn enemies. You know what it's like around here. You've got to be one or the other or you get nowhere. And all the time they're in league. And the joke is, even the top people in the Masons, the Grand Masters or whatever they're called, even the Pope doesn't know! The only ones who know are the Big Ones themselves — and a few people like my Pole. That's why they're after him. That's why he had to get out of Poland. And Argentina! And why he isn't safe even in Rosebery. And that's why you mustn't breathe a word about it to anyone, Dante, or they'd be after us as well."

All this must have made some impression on me

because Johnno begins to enjoy himself. His air of conspiracy, of imminent danger, deepens.

"But that's not the whole thing, even yet. It gets better and better. Because the Big Ones, the ones who really matter, the ones who are pulling the strings and making it all happen — well, what's so enormous is that they aren't big people at all, or not the sort of people you'd *know* were big, with their names in history books or in the newspapers. They're the most inconspicuous people in the world. People you wouldn't tumble to in a million years. Like those old men at the Public Library, f' instance. Who'd suspect one of them? Or Stavros there." Johnno jerks his head towards him, sleeping, or pretending to sleep, with his arms folded on the bar. "It's perfect, don't you see? It's — " he searches for the word, "it's Copernican! Once you've been made to realize it everything suddenly makes sense."

"You believe it then?"

I was thinking of one old man at the library, with half-glasses at the end of his rheumy nose and watery-blue eyes, blood-red at the rims.

"Of course I do. Don't you?"

I shrug my shoulders.

"But it's the only thing that would explain it all," Johnno insists. "The unfairness of things. The absurdity." He gives a big guffaw, then covers his mouth quickly with his hand. Stavros stirs and sits up. Johnno's voice becomes a steady hiss. "Can't you see what a joke it is? Those old men must be pissing themselves, sitting there in the library, watching us swallow all the garbage in those books. History, psycho-analysis, looking at the newspaper headlines! It's one huge, glorious joke." Once again he has to

77

stifle a burst of laughter. "It's cosmic! I knew it was true the moment I heard it. It's the only possible explanation. Only f' God's sake, Dante," he lowers his voice till it is just a breath of air between us, "don't ever, ever tell anyone. Anybody you spoke to might be one of them. Just anybody. And you'd be done for. Pffft! Kaput! It simply isn't worth the risk." He sits back. "All in all, Dante, I think it would be safer if we never mentioned it again. Even to one another."

After the "revelation", and a couple more fiery cognacs, Johnno would be ready for the brothels.

Hidden away behind a ten foot corrugated-iron wall, in one-storeyed weatherboards that were virtually indistinguishable from the spare-parts yards and mechanics' shops of the sleazy areas between the Gardens and Elizabeth Street, the brothels were known, by reputation at least, to every Brisbane schoolboy and exerted an unhealthy influence over the imagination of a good many of the city's most respectable young ladies, who liked to be driven past on their way home from the pictures, to marvel at the crowd of men round the doorway, and to catch, if they were lucky, a glimpse of one of "them", striding about on the footpath in an evening dress slit to the knee or kilted up boldly behind. Mostly, however, they remained invisible behind their wall, and you had to duck your head and go into the little front yard with its geraniums and its trellis of shrivelled vines to see anything more. And even then it might only be the Madam, large and over-dressed in a cane armchair — fanning herself if it was summer, while big moths blundered against a lamp, or warming her feet at a one-bar radiator in Brisbane's brief but chilly winter. The girls kept to their rooms down the hall.

Johnno, on our visits to the brothels, was charm itself — mild-mannered, deferential, gallant. Within minutes of our arrival he and the Madam would be on the best of terms, she chiding him a little when he went too far, he smiling sheepishly, till one of the girls made her appearance at the rails of the one-step verandah and the Madam gave him leave to be off. Without hurry Johnno would excuse himself and drift across.

"Such a charming boy," she would sigh as I shifted from one foot to the other on the stained concrete that was a brilliant green like grass. "And so are you, dear. Only you mustn't be so shy. We're not going to eat you, you know. There's nothing to be afraid of here."

It wasn't true. There was Johnno to be afraid of. And while the Madam settled back plumply to enjoy the scene, I watched Johnno for danger signals. Every now and then the Madam would reach down under her plaited-cane chair, take out a mosquito spray and pump vigorously till a little cloud of droplets hung on the air. "The mozzies are death to me," she would explain delicately. "If there's just one of them within a mile they'll find me out. It's the Gardens being so close." Occasionally in the long silence the animals could be heard from the Gardens menagerie, a sudden screeching of parrots, then the monkeys would start up, shrilling and jabbering, and the hoarse-throated baboons and chimpanzees. If the wind was in the right direction you could even smell them, dark and fetid, unnervingly close. "Horrid, horrid!" the Madam would exclaim, wrinkling the powder of her fine nose. "It's a public disgrace, those poor creatures being locked up like that. I can't bear to think of them."

Meanwhile, Johnno would have gathered quite a group around him. The girls in their kimonos and pallid evening dresses giggled lightly. Madam dozed. I would grow more and more anxious.

And sure enough the good humour would come to an end with a sudden burst of argument. One of the girls would begin to object mildly to something he had said or hinted; this would be followed by further insinuations, bickering, then a full-throated babble, and the Madam, starting awake, would call sweetly: "Now now, kiddies — be nice to one another." The girl would huff and flounce off to her room down the hall. There would be more whispering and giggling, then another outburst, even louder, and the Madam would ease herself out of her chair and go across to see what it was about.

"Now look here. What *is* all this?"

Then protests, recriminations, counter-recriminations, squeals, a full-scale shouting match with slaps, yells, little heel kicks, savage four letter expletives, and Johnno would be whispering at my elbow: "Get ready to run. They're going to call the police!" as with a last vicious stand at the door he would proclaim fiercely: "Get fucked, all youse!" and make off round the corner, with me breathlessly at his heels and the lights of Queen Street swimming dizzily ahead. "Faster!" Johnno would be hissing, "Faster! I can hear them!" Till we were both exhausted and had to pull up in the entrance to a shop.

The police never did come, though Johnno swore he heard the car and would spring into a crouch every time there was a glare of headlamps in the street. And it dawned on me at last that the police, and the chase up Edward Street, like Johnno's drawn-out conversation with the Madam and his carefully calculated scene with the girls, were part of a private and powerfully exciting fantasy that left him panting and streaming with sweat, and which I could not share. The brothels suddenly lost their glamour for me. I became more and more unwilling to go.

"What's the matter with you?" Johnno would demand savagely. "You used to like it." He would sulk and wheedle, and when I did give in at last and agree to go I would throw him into paroxysms of rage by refusing to cooperate in the fantasy at the very moment when his own excitement could brook no qualification.

"For God's sake," he'd yell as I dawdled behind, "for God's sake, Dante, what are you doing? The police are coming. Do you want us to get caught?" I would force myself into a half-hearted trot. And when I slowed again to little more than a fast walk he would lose his head completely: "You bastard, you fucking shit! You *want* us to get caught. They'll be here any minute, I tell you. I can hear the siren!"

But I couldn't make myself run any more. It was too silly. And the game was over anyway. The houses had got to know us and the moment we appeared at the little gate the alarm was raised: "It's him!" and a girl would appear with a bucket of slops. "Come on," she'd challenge, "just you come another step and you'll get the lot, you little bastard."

Johnno was delighted. "You see," he told me,

triumphant. But he kept to the footpath and limited himself to a few desultory insults, urged on by a taxi-load of sailors.

"Get the police," the Madam called from inside, "if he doesn't beat it. Call the dicks!"

Johnno's triumph was complete. "The police, see?" he said defiantly. With a whoop of joy he took to his heels, and on this occasion at least, had me pelting after him. The fantasy was fact at last. He had made it real.

After that we let the brothels lapse. We took to staying at the Greek Club into the early hours of the morning, and after peering through the iron bars of the Gardens, where giant Moreton Bay figs, huge-girthed like elephants, would be emerging out of the bluish dark, and the first animals stirring in their fusty cages, we would part and walk home, or wait at our separate stops for the five o'clock tram.

I liked the city in the early morning. The streets would be wet where one of the big, slow cleaning-machines had been through. In the alleyways between shops florists would be setting out pails of fresh-cut flowers, dahlias and sweet william, or unpacking boxes of gladioli. After Johnno's sullen raging I felt light and free. It was so fresh, so sparkling, the early morning air before the traffic started up; and the sun when it appeared was immediately warm enough to make you sweat. Between the tall city office blocks Queen Street was empty, its tramlines aglow. Despite Johnno's assertion that Brisbane was absolutely the ugliest place in the world, I had the feeling as I walked across deserted intersections, past empty parks with their tropical trees all spiked and sharp-edged in the early sunlight, that it might even be beautiful. But that, no doubt, was light-headedness from lack of sleep or a trick of the dawn.

"What a place!" Johnno would snarl, exasperated by the dust and the packed heat of an afternoon when even the glossy black mynah birds, picking about between the roots of the Moreton Bay figs, were too dispirited to dart out of the way of his boot. "This must be the bloody arsehole of the universe!"

And I had to admit then that it was difficult to see how anything could be made of Brisbane. It was so shabby and makeshift, with its wooden houses perched high on tar-black stilts, its corrugated-iron fences unpainted and rusting, its outdoor lavatories, chicken houses, blocks of uncleared land where the weeds in summer might be six feet tall, a tangle of lantana and morning glory and scraggy sun-flowers. Even in the city itself there were still buildings with first-storey verandahs, and occasionally one of the new facades (all pastel-coloured metal slats) would reveal, if you caught it at the right angle, the weatherboard fabric behind. Nothing seemed permanent here. Brisbane was a huge shanty-town, set down in the middle of nowhere. I was reminded sometimes of ghost-towns in the north that had once had a population of twenty thousand souls and were now completely deserted — the houses one morning simply lifted down from their stumps, loaded on to the back of a lorry, and carted away to create another town a hundred miles off. In my childhood I had often seen houses being carried through the streets, creaking and swaying on the back of a truck. It wouldn't have surprised anyone, I think, to wake up one morning and find that Brisbane too had died overnight. Its corrugated iron would be sold off for scrap. The weatherboard houses would rot in the damp, be carted away, or fall victim to the voraciousness of white ants. Animals would nest in upturned water tanks.

And who, Johnno asked, would know the difference? Brisbane was nothing: a city that blew neither hot nor cold, a place where nothing happened, and where nothing ever would happen, because it had no soul. People suffered here without significance. It was too mediocre even to be a province of hell. It would have defeated even Baudelaire! A place where poetry could never occur.

Perhaps.

"The trouble with you, Dante," Johnno told me severely, "is you're a romantic! All you see is what you feel. Before you know what's happened you'll be married and have a job in the Public Library and an ugly squalling dimply called Wayne. You'll end up with a paragraph in *The Courier-Mail:* distinguished local man dies of heart-attack at One Tree Hill."

But the trouble with me on other occasions was that I wasn't romantic enough. I stood off and refused to get involved. I had too much irony, too much common sense. I was cut off from what Johnno called "life" — though what Johnno called life bore an uncanny resemblance, it seemed to me, to what the rest of us called "literature". He had recently been burying himself in the Russia of Dostoievski, and had come more and more, with his shaggy head and big-boned, ungainly gestures, to resemble Rogozin of *The Idiot*, giving way when he was drunk (after two beers, that is) to savage rages.

I would watch him working himself up to it, a bout of his "Nordic madness". He would sit looking gloomy and enormous, calling up stormclouds as he sucked on what might have been a raging tooth, an iceberg the size of a cathedral. His northern blood boiled at this temperature, at this time of the year, ten thousand miles and as many centuries south of its starting point; his blue eyes smoked. The Long Bar at the Criterion at four-thirty on a summer afternoon was the scene of terrible carnage, the dead lay strewn across traffic intersections and metal trams were charred and buckled, pouring out sparks. Then utter calm. His eyes would be clearest icy-blue, dazzling without depth, and he would be pure again, cleaned out and calm. On such occasions, I came to realize, he was in pursuit of his "soul", which he would suddenly have lost contact with. It was inclined to wander. Locating itself, it seemed, in his funny-bone, or the hollows of a molar, or in an appendix that flared and puffed up like a dragon on its island, then slept again for another seven years. There were days when he lost track of it altogether. He would barge about a room as if some invisible air current were tossing him at will. The soul would have broken out of his body altogether and set up residence in a one-bar radiator where it glowed with menace, or gone buzzing about over the treetops in a model aeroplane that some schoolkid was playing out on a string. He would rage, glare murderously, and for all my scepticism, I was terrified. He seemed quite capable one day of running amok like the Jugoslav and killing half a dozen strangers with a tomahawk, just to prove to himself (or to me) that his anguish was real. People

85

began to warn me against him. "One day that Johnno will go beserk. If you happen to be around he'll put an axe through your head," they'd tell me, "or slip a breadknife into you." It seemed entirely possible. But I believed somehow in my own immunity. Johnno's rages always broke beyond me. It was as if, in his cities of the plain, I was always to be the one just man for whom all the rest are saved.

He had one other close friend at this period, who was always being held up to me as the opposite of everything I stood for (I had never seen him in fact, Johnno took great pains to keep us apart), the real soul-mate of his rages and aspirations — a medical student called Bill Mahoney. Bill was a real terror, a dionysian whirlwind, a stick of dynamite, a Nachaev. There was nothing Bill wouldn't do. He was a killer, an assassin, who had conscientiously rid himself of every bourgeois squeamishness, every bookish sentimentality. Bill was an exterminating angel. And to look at him you'd think butter wouldn't melt in his mouth. That was the whole point of course. A real spy had to be unrecognizable. An exterminating angel must look and act like a bank clerk. Bill's plan was to work himself towards the centre of society, conforming with it, cooperating with it at every point, in order to bring it down. In the meantime he and Johnno were putting themselves through a crash course in the disintegration of consciousness. It was a systematic programme. You began with something simple, like an act of theft, then went on step by step to the end. Destroying the myth was a process like any other.

And the end?

That, of course, was just the sort of question I

would ask. Who could know what the end would be, when all the myths had dissolved like so many ghostly chains and we were free to be ourselves?

Johnno had embarked in the meantime on a quite prodigious programme of shoplifting.

With a daring so outrageous that he was never even questioned, let alone caught, he would sweep through Barker's Bookstore picking up books from left and right till the pile was so high under his chin that he could barely see. On past the cash desk, staggering slightly. Out into Edward Street. Where he would tumble the whole pile into a swing-top litter bin.

"Jesus!" he would whisper, with the sweat pouring off him and his legs weak with excitement. And the pure exhilaration of it would last all the way up Queen Street.

"There are too many books anyway," he would tell me fiercely. "And cars!" (glaring at the traffic as we pushed across against the lights). "And toasters, Mixmasters, washing machines!" He would have walked off with a washing machine if he'd been able to manage it; staggered up Queen Street and toppled it over Victoria Bridge into the river. "The trouble with you, Dante, is you're intimidated by objects, you know that? I bet you wince every time the spine cracks on a book. You're a complete product of the consumer society. A credit to the power of advertising!"

But worse even than my respect for property, or my rationalism, was my contemptible sense of humour.

Wandering idly round Barker's, flicking through art books or the new poetry, I would suddenly come upon Johnno in the mystical act of making his first theft, his face trancelike and distant as his right hand hovered over one of the tables, hesitating fastidiously between Somerset Maugham, for whom he had a particular loathing, and Daphne du Maurier. Entirely solemn and engaged. And as our eyes met, briefly, what he recognized in mine would drive him to raving distraction. A sense of humour of my sort, he told me, was disgusting, mere bourgeois self-protectiveness, and a sure sign of bad faith!

His own commitments were never anything but wholeheartedly complete.

Under the influence of his Russian reading he had discovered a sudden need to abase himself, like Dmitri Karamazov, before a holy man, and had made tentative moves toward the Russian Orthodox Church. He consulted the phone book, made one or two anonymous calls, even sent them a breathless and ecstatically confessional letter. But the local Russians, mostly White, who had found their way to Australia via Shanghai and were terrified of being followed, took fright at Johnno's approach, suspected he was some sort of agent or a local crackpot and threatened him with the police. He took savagely against them and turned to the Greeks. After all, as everyone knew, the Greek Orthodox Church was older, purer than the Russian, holier even if the truth was known. From Stavros the barman at the Club he got the address of an Orthodox priest, and set out early one morning, after an all-night preparation, for the house in the West End, to abase himself and be purified.

He used to tell the story of what happened then with great booming guffaws; but at the time, I'm sure, he was deadly serious. His appearance in the little front garden off the tramline, wild-eyed, shaggy, must have terrified the priest's wife, who opened the door in her apron and with a squalling half-naked child on her hip. She spoke no English, and could make nothing of Johnno's extravagant gesturing. When the priest came out in his shirt-sleeves (he was in the middle of breakfast), Johnno knelt, kissed the cuffs of his trousers and then (to the priest's considerable consternation) lay full-length on the path between the cannas and beat his brow upon the stone.

"What do you do here?" the priest shouted, flinging his hands about and making apologetic and helpless gestures towards the passers-by, who had come from the tramstop and were peering in over the picket fence. The baby squalled, the wife had hysterics, Johnno moaned and beat his brow. "This is a madman," the priest explained in panic. "He is unknown to me. Quite definitely unknown."

"Forgiveness," Johnno wailed, beginning, now that the whole thing had turned into a farce, to enjoy himself, and determined to make trouble for that "shit of a priest".

In the end there was a brawl. The priest· began kicking and demanding that he get up, and Johnno bit his leg. Someone scrambled over the fence to part them and Johnno was at last driven off, but came back to shout obscenities and throw clods of dirt at the priest's windows till he came out and threatened him with the police. Johnno was incensed. All the priest had cared about was what the neighbours thought. He had offered to abase himself and they had turned the whole thing into a public scandal. Anyway (he would be shaken by an outburst of giggles) what was the use of abasing yourself on the earth when the earth itself, at this particular point, was so utterly un-holy? There had been ants on that path. They'd swarmed all over him. Who ever heard of Holy West End? As he'd always insisted, it was a place where real anguish was the subject for nothing but the most disgusting comedy.

Even, as it turned out, the anguish of the heart.

VIII

Johnno's being in love, desperately, hopelessly, towards the end of his final year, came as a complete surprise to me. For a long time I didn't even suspect. He seemed quieter, that's all. Then one night he opened up and raged. He had been caught while his resistance was low by the most insidious bloody madness of them all, the subtlest and most self-destructive invention of the whole rag-bag of bourgeois delusions, romantic fucking love! What's more the girl was an idiot. A silly bitch of a librarian who read comics off-duty because she "worked all day with books", and had nothing to talk about but horses, weekends at the Coast, and how many of the sons of big station-owners up north she had been "practically engaged to".

Her name was Binkie. For nearly a year, perhaps more, she must have been to Johnno what she was to me, one of the liveliest girls at the parties we went to, the dark, tomboyish daughter of a Mackay cane miller, who drank rum and coke and had a deep, thick voice the colour, I always thought, of molasses. When she was very drunk she'd get one of us to ring long-distance to check on some boy back home who was her current fiance, and often enough the only person who would do it was me.

"He's two-timing me, the bastard!" she'd whisper

over my shoulder as I waited for the number to answer.

Then when there was a voice at last: "That's his mother. Tell her you're one of his old school mates from Churchie." Then darkly, as the voice at the other end explained that Ross or Brian or Murray was out for the evening: "I wonder what he's up to the two-timing bastard. Out with the boys my foot!"

She was the girl who introduced us to "Bottles", a deadly game that we played late on in the evening, when people had mostly gone off home or drifted into empty bedrooms. We would stand in a circle round the table with full glasses before us of whatever we were drinking — beer, sherry, rum and coke — and number off: *one two three* etc., fast around the circle. Only for every number containing a four or a seven or any multiple of either you substituted the word "Bottles". And if you hesitated, or missed, you drank off the entire contents of your glass.

Binkie played the game with a mad intensity.

"Faster," she'd yell, "you're giving yourself time to think, it's not fair."

"Forty-six."

"Bottles."

"Bottles."

"Bottles."

"Fifty."

"Fifty-one."

"Fif . . ."

"No no, you missed," she'd cry triumphantly, "fifty-two is four times thirteen. Down the hatch! Now come on. Faster!"

"Fifty-three."

"Bottles."

"Fifty-five."

"Fift . . . "

"No no, bottles! Fifty-six is bottles. What's the matter with everyone? I'm going to win again."

I don't know when Binkie stopped being the "Bottles girl" for Johnno and became something more. I don't even know when they saw one another, or how long it lasted, or if there was anything to it even, except in Johnno's overwrought imagination. I was having my own problems, in the form of a plump, good-natured girl called Rhoda. Her father owned a chain of second-hand car yards and her house, a big two-storeyed mansion overlooking the river, was just a stone's throw from ours on Kingsford Smith Drive. For two or three months I used to meet her when she was off-duty from nursing school, and at the weekend, when her parents were away, we would sit in a swing on her front verandah watching the spidery lights on the river and listening, in the dark, to the put-put of fishing boats going out to the Bay. Then suddenly, without warning, it was over. Rhoda's father disapproved of me, I was a Catholic. I prepared to argue: I wasn't a Catholic at all, I didn't believe, I hadn't been to church since I was fifteen, what did her father mean? But the state of my beliefs wasn't really the question. Rhoda's father had promised her a Californian hardtop for her twenty-first. And, well —. She looked dewy-eyed and regretful, but I saw immediately that I couldn't compete. I spent several evenings moping about town and examining my rival in display windows. It was beautiful, I had to agree. It cost just over a thousand pounds, though her father, I realized, would get discount for being in the trade. A thousand pounds, minus twenty-five per cent. Say seven hundred and fifty. I nursed my wounds and told myself, stoically, that it wasn't every young man of just twenty who knew his price on the open market. We remained friends for a while and continued to turn up at the same weekend parties, but it never really worked and she was tactful enough to drop me, firmly, before the hardtop actually materialized as more than a shadow between us. I never saw her again.

Binkie had been good to me through all this. She knew what was going on and she encouraged me to talk about it. Having just broken it off with Stuart, or Douglas, or whatever the boy in the north was called, she was inclined to be bitterly humorous.

"Men are such shits," she would say, leaning on one elbow and shaking her head. "Do you know he got some girl pregnant on a football trip and actually *married* her?" She drained off the last of her rum and coke. Then seeing my hangdog look, leaned across and put her hand on mine. "Oh poor Dante! I'd forgotten. Well, I suppose some women are too!"

One morning early, after a party, I was walking her to the first tram. It was nearly dawn. We had stopped halfway across Grey Street Bridge to peer over the concrete balustrade to where tramps slept on the tufty piece of waste-ground under the approach.

"I trailed one of those old fellows from the library once," Binkie told me dreamily. "There was a whole colony of them — they had a fire in a kerosene tin and one of them was playing an accordion."

I had become aware, while she was talking, that someone was following us. He had stopped just out of sight, at the springing of the arch, and was eavesdropping on us. I saw his shadow briefly in the glow

94

of the lamps. I said nothing to Binkie, not wanting to alarm her, and we walked on. When we stopped again to listen to the starlings that had suddenly begun to twitter, thousands and thousands of them it seemed, invisible in the milky, lamplit air, the figure moved again and stood right in our path, so that Binkie saw him too. The sun came up, and with it a fog that suddenly thickened and rose off the river in a dense white cloud. We were all shrouded in it. The starlings twittered. Binkie caught my arm briefly, then relaxed.

She took a step forward and called angrily through the fog. "I might have known it was you. What do you want now?"

Johnno looked big and foolish in the half-light. His shirt half out of his trousers, his hair ruffled, he was pretending, not very successfully, to be drunk. Binkie made a little gesture of desperation and went past him. I hesitated for a moment, and Johnno, seeing the difficulty I was in, shrugged his shoulders and turned slightly to let me pass. As I did so he laid his hand briefly on my shoulder, as if to absolve me of any complicity in the affair. It was strictly between Binkie and himself.

When I caught up with her she was shaking, though with the first touch of sunlight the day's warmth had come. We walked on and I could hear him a dozen or so paces behind, whistling tunelessly in the fog.

Suddenly Binkie turned on her heel: "Go to hell," she shouted. "Why can't you behave like other people? You know I don't want you. Just piss off!"

He had stopped, and gradually I could make out his bulk. The sun was lighting the edge of a great curve of stone beyond him and the milky fog was beginning to drift and go thin. In a moment it would lift altogether and we would be face to face in the early morning sunlight.

"Oh, come *on*," Binkie said miserably, hauling at my elbow. "Ignore him." And she began to walk off.

"Are you OK?" I asked, uneasily aware that it would be simpler, later, if nothing had passed between us, but feeling that I couldn't go without speaking to him.

"I'm OK," he said.

He turned back, and I walked with Binkie into the wide crossroads in front of the bridge and silently under the fig trees along Petrie Terrace, beside the railway yards, where the first trucks were beginning to shunt and the cattle could be heard stirring, bellowing in their yards.

"Damn him!" Binkie said fiercely. "Damn him, damn him! He's driving me up the wall."

Johnno never mentioned this incident and never referred in the following weeks to the fact that Binkie and I were friends, or lovers perhaps, for all he knew. He was away for most of that summer, mapping Lake Manchester for his geology thesis, and when we saw one another briefly he was no different. Gentler if anything. It was Binkie who talked now and kept me, somehow, involved. She had a flat along the river at New Farm and I went there after work to play knock-about games of tennis on the tumbledown court or to swim in the tepid swimming-pool.

"For God's sake," Binkie would say, half-laughing at it all, "he's trying to educate me! Look at this."

It was Lermontov's *A Hero of our Time*. He had also sent her on other occasions Tolstoi's *Resurrection*, Goethe's *Elective Affinities* and a glossy presentation recording of Mozart's *Requiem.*

"Honestly, Dante, I just don't know what to do. It's getting me down. It's so — " she gave one of her dark little chuckles, that was like sudden bubbles in a vat, it was so rich and dark with suggestion. " — so silly! I mean, I'm not *altogether* stupid you know."

She sat in a window-seat amid a scatter of stockings, clothespegs, old copies of *Harpers* and *Vogue.* I was suddenly swept by a familiar emotion.

"You're lovely, Binkie," I said, and reached out for her fingers.

She made a wry face.

"Oh, don't you start, Dante!"

And it was enough, at that moment, to turn away the brief possibility. She looked out at the gathering dusk.

"Do you see that jacaranda down there? Well he stands there sometimes, all night. I have to go right past him on my way to the tram in the morning. If someone takes me out he suddenly turns up at the next table and just sits there. The boys I go out with must think I'm an absolute nut. We get to a place, sit down, order, and the next minute I want to go somewhere else. He's driving me crazy! He really is!" She got up and started to pick stockings up off the carpet and roll them ready to wash. Then she stopped, thought a moment, and collected one by one the magazines. "I suppose in the end," she said, as if she had already started to pack, "I'll have to go home for a while. Till he leaves."

Johnno was leaving in February for the Congo. He had a job there and had already signed the contract and applied for a passport. But if Binkie, who wasn't entirely displeased I thought to be the centre of all this, had decided it was love that was driving him out of the country, she would have been sadly disappointed. Love was only part of it. This, for Johnno, was to be the great escape. His break at last into perfect freedom.

"I'm going to shit this bitch of a country right out of my system," he told me fiercely. "Twenty fucking years! How long will it take me, do you think, to shit out every last trace of it? At the end of every seven years you're completely new — did you know that? New fingernails, new hair, new cells. There'll be nothing left in me of bloody Australia. I'll be transmuted. I'll say to myself every morning as I squat on the dunny, there goes another bit of Australia. That was Wilson's Promontory. That was Toowong. Whoosh, down the plughole! And at the end of seven years I'll have squeezed the whole fucking continent out through my arsehole. I'll have got rid of it for ever. All *this*." His wild glance took in Queen Street at four in the afternoon, with the newsboys innocently shouting the racing results, and women shoppers, with no conception of the fate Johnno had in store for them, shifting wearily from foot to foot in the islands between the traffic. It seemed a large task for one man to accomplish. Even in a lifetime. Let alone seven years.

IX

All that month before Johnno left for the Congo it
rained. Not the ordinary rains of February, the sharp
midsummer thunderstorms that gather punctually at
four, roll their bruise-coloured clouds across the
range, explode, bubble for an hour or so in gutters,
then vanish. This was *rain*: slow, steady, interminable.
The city's vegetation stirred and swayed like sea-
weed, and we sweated in our plastic raincoats, wetter
inside than out. Brisbane had seen nothing like it
since the '93 flood, when old Victoria Bridge, a
substantial iron affair, had broken up under the
pressure of the debris and been swept down-stream,
and the Queensland Navy's only gunboat was left
high and dry in the Botanical Gardens.

Nothing quite so historic happened this time. But
each night after work, with the bridge lamps casting
their yellow glare far into the sky, crowds gathered
on the footwalks of the bridge and on the high
embankment along North Quay to see the river come
swirling down between the iron pylons of the bridge
and to point out to one another the strange cargo it
carried: huge tree-trunks that strained and splintered
where they struck, chicken-coops, water tanks,
butter-boxes, even sometimes an odd piece of
furniture, a genoa velvet lounge-chair, for example,
that bucked about on the surface of the water like

the Tilt-a-Whirl at the National Show. And other things even more wonderful to city eyes: dead cattle with their feet in the air; great islands of waterlilies where the field creatures, bushrats and lizards, swarmed as on a raft. And leaving the river swollen and brown for days afterwards, whole acres of rich Brisbane Valley topsoil. A farmer standing here might have seen two or three of his best paddocks go past. The river, usually placid enough with its rainbow-slick of oil and its bubbles of ferment popping in the heat, boiled up now into lighted peaks like the sea, and its roar could be heard from tramstops half a block away. Twice daily, with the tides, it rose up through the drains into low-lying suburbs and left its ripple mark on the walls. People went out in rowing boats to see a dressing-table drawer full of stinking mud or a dozen catfish gasping in a bath. It was a month of wonders.

For Johnno it was time out of life — a three-week no-man's-land. His papers were signed, he had his air ticket, the vaccination scratch on his arm had swelled and scabbed. All he had to do now was sit it out till his plane left.

He was sentimental and bad tempered. "Let's go and visit the Dutchman," he'd say. Till I reminded him that he had already told the Dutchman he was a bastard, and always had been, and that he was glad to see the last of him. Too late for the Dutchman!

And for everyone else he knew. With a whole week to go he had insulted most of his friends, made himself *persona non grata* at all the places he wanted to keep fond memories of, and was reduced to sitting damply in the Long Bar at the Criterion, while rain played on the lead-light windows over his shoulder

100

and I — the last companion — sipped my shandy and pretended that the silences between us were filled with deep emotion, or at any rate, deep thoughts.

We must have done *something* in those weeks. Gone to the pictures or poked about the bookshops. But all I remember at this distance is the bluish gloom of the Long Bar and Johnno's rages, round four o'clock, when it began to fill with sober-suited lawmen from the Inns of Court. Occasionally, if we survived the hour when the bar was dense and noisy with intruders, we would still be there at half past six or seven; Johnno a bit low by then, and inclined to be sulky rather than boisterous, I (a good half-dozen long drinks behind) at an indeterminate point between light headedness and the queasy suspicion that I might, before the night was out, be sick.

On one such occasion, when the flood was at its peak, we walked up Queen Street with the crowd and made our way, slipping and sliding on the wet tracks, down the steep embankment north of the bridge. A wooden ramp ran down to the water, one of the Grammar School rowing pontoons, and we sat there for a while and watched the lights of the Blue Moon Skating Rink on the far bank play red and green across the waves. It was just after eight. Behind us was the verandah of the O'Connor Boathouse where we had sometimes gone to dances. On the foot-walk of the bridge, immediately above, I could see rows of umbrellas gleaming under the lamps. Though it was barely drizzling now; just a fine silver mist that made the neons, TIGER BATTERIES, EAT MORE FISH, swim a little in the air.

Suddenly, without warning, Johnno had staggered to his feet and was hauling off his shirt.

"What are you doing?" I asked foolishly.

His shirt fell on the boards beside me, his shoes were off, he was slipping his trousers down over his knees.

"I'm going in."

He rolled his socks off and went to the edge of the ramp in his sagging underpants.

"Are you coming?" He stood there, impatient. "Well, are you?"

Silhouetted for a moment against the play of lights on the water, he shivered at the first touch of coldness at his heels, then jack-knifed neatly and was gone.

I was stunned. It had all happened so quickly. I got to my feet and peered into the darkness. He was nowhere to be seen. Of course I should call for help, he would probably be drowned. Struck on the head by a tree-trunk or dragged down by weeds. Only I felt so silly. I stood peering and the river thundered. There was absolutely no sign of him. I cleared my throat, preparing to call. Then about ten yards offshore, his head appeared, bobbing about in a kaleidoscope of scarlet and green.

"It's great," he shouted, waving a white arm. "Come on in. Piker!" He struck out into midstream, turning skilfully to avoid the debris, and was carried down towards the pylons of the bridge. Then began to swim strongly back again. "Come on in!" he yelled, his voice high against the roaring of the waves. "Piker, Dante! Piker!"

Obviously he was in no danger. I sat with my knees drawn up at the edge of the ramp while he tumbled about in the lights, and began to feel resentful. People up on the bridge had picked him out now. I could see them pointing. Maybe they would call for help, it would serve him right! He was showing off. I sat and sulked. It was too late now to get myself out of my clothes and follow. It would be too deliberate, nothing at all like his free, unselfconscious plunge. And besides, I would have to appear in an hour or so at my aunt's house, where the family were at dinner. How could I turn up stinking of riverwater, having dried off on my shirt, and with mud in my hair?

"Piker," Johnno taunted in the darkness.

Sullenly, I waited on the sidelines for him to come out.

It would be fitting, I suppose, if that were my last memory of Johnno in those early years. But it is not. There was a whole week left before his flight, and when the weather cleared at last we moved out of the Criterion to the garden of the Lands Office, and even, once, took a trip to Lone Pine, where Johnno had himself photographed with a koala. Our final meeting (we both thought of it as that) was at Littleboys Coffee Lounge above King George Square, a cosy old-fashioned place not much bigger than a suburban living-room, from which there was a view of fountains that never played, an equestrian statue of King George V, and the sparking-poles of passing trams. You could sit all afternoon over a single coffee at Littleboys, till the waitress appeared at five-thirty with the evening menu (cover charge two shillings) and it was time to leave.

We were heavily aware, both of us, that this was the end of something and we wanted it to go well.

But for once, curiously, we had nothing to say. Johnno presented me with a going-away gift, a book of translations from Rimbaud, which he assured me he had not "organized", and we watched a shower skitter over the rooftops, making them gleam for a moment in the sun. Johnno tried to liven things up a bit by producing a rage: against Brisbane, against Australia; but his denunciation of the city, delivered from that modest elevation, had about as much effect on the crowds below as the passing sunshower.

"You'd need a fucking bomb," he hissed bitterly. "And even then they wouldn't notice. They'd decide someone had let off a particularly thunderous fart and pretend they hadn't heard."

A long silence. It was just after three. Johnno threw one leg heavily over the other and stared out the window. He narrowed his eyes, and might have been flicking idle pebbles across a pool, far away in the centre of himself, the hard pebbles skipping over the surface of the afternoon, faster, more spiteful, closer to the passing heads. He swung his leg back again, sighed, and announced abruptly: "I'd better be getting home, Dante. I really had. I've still got my packing to do." He paused. "And I've got one or two — aunts to visit." He included other activities in a vague, unfinished gesture that appropriately enough caught the eye of the waitress, who came up swiftly with the bill.

Outside in the street we walked uncomfortably towards Johnno's tramstop. I tried to think of something to say, or do, that would be adequate to the occasion, adequate to what I would want later to recall. But what? We were almost at the corner. Suddenly I was caught in a Dostoievskian bearhug.

"Goodbye Dante," Johnno sobbed, close to my ear, and he was gone — dodging off through the crowd to where his tram was pulling in on the far side of the lights.

He left me in a daze. It had all happened so quickly. People were staring. And his tram had rattled past before I even thought to wave!

Awful! Awful! Awful! I burned with embarrassment. I had just stood there, stiff and unresponsive. Maybe in the shock of the moment I had even pushed him away. That would be typical! I tried to recall the moment. What was the last thing I had been thinking before it happened? But it was all a blur. If only it could happen over again! Only *slowly*, so that I wouldn't be caught unprepared. I saw clearly how Johnno, on his journey home, would be reliving his half of the experience. Awful! I had never been so ashamed in my life.

Still suffering, I wandered along Queen Street, trying to play it over in my memory so that I could be sure of how it *had* been. Maybe I hadn't pushed him away after all.

It must have been at the Black Cat corner that I looked up briefly out of my misery and saw — my God! it was Johnno, five yards off, coming right past me. He must have seen me at the same moment. Grinning sheepishly, making a little ducking movement with his head, he passed in the crowd, and in less than a minute there were a hundred strangers between us.

Unwilling to risk yet another ghostly encounter, I took the first tram to the Valley and spent the hours till tea-time at the Civic, watching an ancient western and four episodes of an even more ancient serial.

X

Africa was a long way off. Johnno went to work at a copper mine on the borders of the Congo and messages from him, apocalyptic announcements on a postcard, were few and far between, the outcome of drunken weekends in Salisbury or Johannesburg when he might have felt a twinge of nostalgia for our nights out, or tragic moments on the morning after when he would be bothered again with the "soul".

Scrawled across a postcard in his big loose hand, these messages were too cryptic, too infrequent, to tell me much of what he was feeling. *"Truth is blue, the colour of all hangovers,"* they might announce. Or *"Wer, wenn ich schriee, hoerte mich denn aus den Engel Ordnungen?"* The moments they sprang from were all extreme. He felt the need to reach out only when he was either desperately miserable or in some sort of ecstasy, and I knew, as he must have, that by the time his words reached me, five thousand miles away, as I was rushing out of the house for a tram, his mood would already be gone — replaced by whatever it was his silences represented: long stretches of sitting alone in a tent at the end of nowhere, with nothing but his native boys and his books, or weeks of tramping across country in the sun.

About that he had nothing to tell. Though he did write sometimes about the books.

He had them crated out to camp headquarters every six months, from Blackwells in Oxford: Schopenhauer, Berdiaev, Wittgenstein, Bonhöffer, Sartre — not to mention the novelists old and new, from Madame de Lafayette to Musil and Kazantzakis Since he never, so far as I knew, *kept* a book (as objects he despised them, they were just receptacles to be emptied of their contents and thrown away) I used to imagine him sitting in a pair of faded khaki shorts on a camp stool, somewhere on Lake Victoria; flamingoes would be flocking away into the sun and big game animals swaying across the horizon; Johnno, swatting insects with one hand, thumbing pages with the other, would be hunched over one of his newly arrived consignments, and as he turned the last page of each crisp, new volume he would toss it lightly over his shoulder, where it would sink, with a few gobbling sounds, into primeval African mud. When his three-year contract was up he was off to Europe. What he was acquiring in Africa (and disposing of in its torpid lakes) was "civilization". No longer a barbarian, he would arrive in Europe with six thousand pounds in his pocket and the capacity for living at last among civilized men. He urged me to give up shadow boxing in the suburbs of limbo and follow him before it was too late.

For some reason I declined to take his advice. Though almost everyone I knew had left Brisbane now, I stubbornly hung on. Binkie passed through on her way to the National Library in Canberra, and the next I heard she was engaged again — this time to a doctor whom she would marry "almost absolutely immediately, before he gets away". People took jobs with the Public Service and were sent interstate. Or they got scholarships and went to Europe. I went to B.P. as a statistics clerk, sinking week by week into a despondency deeper than anything I had ever known or thought possible.

It wasn't the job. I had found that by instinct. It was the only one I could have lasted in. It suited my mood. I spent eight hours a day checking dockets from service stations in the remotest parts of the state against their monthly sales-sheets; processing countless gallons of B.P. super and standard, 30 oil, 40 oil, and Viscostatic, and balancing sales against returns to see that the empty drums were all accounted for and hadn't gone loose somewhere in the paddocks beyond Roma, where they might be used illegally as a water-butt or split in two to make feeding-bins, or be rusting away in the stomachs of omnivorous goats. When I had done a good-sized pile of stocksheets I made a "bundle", by skewering the corner with a slotted knife, inserting a pin, and then beating the points down with the knife handle. Half a dozen hard, vicious blows that set every tack and bottle on my desk jumping and shaking like the devil was in them. The devil, in fact, was in me. "Making a bundle" was one way of driving him out and I could imagine the look on my own face from the looks I observed on the faces of my fellow workers — mouths set hard, eyes glinting, as they clasped the knife-end of their "bundler" and hammered hard with the wood. At the end of the accounting month I collected the files I had been working on over the past thirty days, loaded them on a trolley, took them

108

to the roof in a special lift, and tipped the whole hundred-weight or more down a chute that dropped them seven storeys into a basement incinerator.

I went from B.P. to a coaching college.

All one scorching summer I blazed from suburb to suburb on a Fanny Barnet two-stroke to coach failed students in English, Latin, and what I could remember (or swot up overnight) of my pure maths.

And still I hung on. I was determined, for some reason, to make life reveal whatever it had to reveal *here*, on home ground, where I would recognize the terms. In Europe, I thought, some false glamour might dazzle me out of any recognition of what was common and ordinary.

I spent long hours at night along the piers at Hamilton, talking to the fishermen and picking up, as I talked, a little of their patience as they waited hopelessly, in those oily waters, for cat-fish to bite. At weekends I took my bike to the Coast. Nothing extraordinary ever deigned to reveal itself to me. Several times I thought I was in love — once, not so briefly, with a boy from Sarina and we spent a good deal of our time riding suicidally into the darkness off country roads, seeking some sort of romantic dissolution, and skidded often enough for me to be left with half a dozen minor burns. But what remains with me most strongly are impressions I can barely have noticed at the time. They were just part of the background to whatever else I was feeling: the low bridge at Tallabudgera as I rode into a mist so dense in the early morning sunlight that it was like riding upward into cloud — then a flash as it lifted, and the broad creek rippled to the sea. Or a stunned hammerhead one afternoon between two sandbanks off Point Danger, its belly pearl-like as it turned and turned in the shallow water while a fisherman plugged at it with a .303. Two years drifted by, in which I learned nothing, it seemed, and certainly achieved nothing. I had five jobs, two serious near-misses on the motorbike, and was twenty-three.

When I think back to that period now I wonder how I can have endured so long the disappointment of my own expectations. All my prospects had simply shrivelled into nothing like burning cellophane. All those inner resources I had been cultivating turned into a vacuum inside me. I watched boys I had known at school get Rhodes Scholarships to Oxford or play their way into the state cricket selections, and found myself entirely without envy of them — entirely un-pricked by my mother's pointed enquiry, as she regarded their photograph in *The Courier-Mail*, whether that wasn't So-and-So who was at Grammar with me, wasn't *he* doing well! People I had known forever paired off and got married. I bought them watersets or electric jugs and failed to turn up at the reception. Someone a year younger that I was (hope-less I had always thought him when we were at school) found uranium on his father's cattle station and was a millionaire twice over before he was twenty-two. What astonished me, I think, was to discover that I was entirely without ambition. I found no need in myself to succeed on these terms. I wasn't suffering — though I couldn't have been called happy. I was in good health. My life was easy, undemanding. I didn't even have the comfort of being a victim. I was simply immobilized from within.

XI

Johnno had been in Paris for over a year, teaching English to private pupils (mostly Bulgarians as far as I could gather) and giving conversation lessons two afternoons a week at the Lycée Henri Quatre. He had a mistress — after all, this was Paris — and it was to her address in the Rue Fossé St. Bernard that I sent my letters and the telegram announcing my arrival.

I rode up in the train from Naples through the lovely Italian countryside. It was spring already and the terraces between the farmhouses with their faded green shutters were foamy with peach and almond blossom; sharp verticals of cypress pointed to a clear blue sky. I felt vaguely disturbed that Europe might after all be about to do what Brisbane had refused to do, break the spell that had been over me. We crossed the Alps in a series of thunderous tunnels between sun-struck peaks, and when we emerged again it was into the depths of winter — row upon row of poplars that looked, against the dirty clouds, like witches' broomsticks upended and stuck savagely into the earth. Paris in the late afternoon was low, grey, smog-ridden. What impressed me most, I think, was the cats cradle of television aerials and the greasiness of the cobbles as we flashed past cafes already lighted, at four in the afternoon, behind smoky glass. When I got off at last at the Gare de Lyon and Johnno wasn't there to meet me I was already colder and more miserable than I had ever felt in my life before. O Brisbane! O Baudelaire!

For an hour or so I simply wandered about in the station, unable to think what I should do or where I should go. I was hungry, but too self-conscious to enter one of the station restaurants, and unwilling as yet to face the city outside. I found a street map and located the Fossé St. Bernard. It was about a mile off, as far as I could tell by spanning my hand across the city and allowing for kilometres, on the far side of the Seine. I planned an indirect but unmistakable route towards it along the main boulevards and set off in my inadequate clothes through the late afternoon drizzle.

The concierge at the Fossé St. Bernard was suspicious and not inclined to follow my French.

She knew of no Australian gentleman. She had never heard of a Monsieur Johnson. And Madame Bousson, who was away in Corsica, did *not* have a club foot! I cursed Johnno's preference for the sentimentally bizarre. (I should have recognized his picture of Madame Bousson from a minor tale of Maupassant.) Still, there *was* a Madame Bousson, and when I showed one of Johnno's postcards the concierge shrugged her shoulders, disappeared into her hutch under the stairs and came back peering over her spectacles at a scrap of grey note-paper. I recognized Johnno's hand immediately. He would be waiting for me, sometime round eight, at the Café Bonaparte.

But the monsieur who had left the note for me was not, the concierge insisted, called Johnson and he was not an Australian. He was a Scot!

112

I hurried back, still keeping to the boulevards but already feeling cheered. In all the cafes now the tables were crowded with girls in suede jackets and long blond hair à la Bardot and young men with beards cut square under the cheek bones and bare upper lips. Older men, with plump shaven cheeks, any one of whom might have been Jean Paul Sartre, talked animatedly behind the glass with little soundless ploppings of the mouth, like carp, and there was a good deal of steam and intensity. The intellectual life of la Belle France was going on all around me. An amoured car swung into the street, nearly catching me as I stepped off the pavement on the wrong side, and one or two passers-by catcalled, then sprinted off into the dark. On the walls, on the footpath, everywhere, there were slogans in white paint: ACTION FRANCAISE, or a hammer and sickle, or the General's two-barred Cross of Lorraine. Under the iron street-lamps, with their circles of delicate filigree round the base, tramps began to gather, great crowds of men with beards and floppy boots, who lay down on the pavement where the hot air comes up in a blast from the Metro, side by side in their rags, looking oddly, as the steam began to rise off them, as if they were being immolated on communal pyres. In the big shop windows round the Madeleine plaster figures glowed in a world of racehorses and light red bicycles. There were leafy branches overhead, as they gestured from wrought-iron benches and garden chairs, in parks that were already bursting into spring. In front of one such window, its shelves brightly lit with rows of fashion shoes in every conceivable colour — scarlet, beige, emerald, yellow, mauve — an old woman stood with her hand out, begging, shifting from one bare horny foot to the other in the cold.

I found Johnno walking up and down the cobbled square, a monk-like figure with the cowl of his duffle-coat drawn forward against the rain.

"Dante!" he exclaimed in a rather pinched voice that I would never have recognized, and which turned out later to be Johnno's version of Scots. (No one, it seemed, would employ an Australian to teach them English. It was the accent. *Effroyable*!) He clasped me formally, in the French manner, and drew me to one of the tables under the awning. "You went to the Fossé, then."

I didn't want to complain: "Yes I did. I thought you lived there. The concierge —"

Johnno lifted his shoulders slightly and his lids drooped. A gesture expressing a great deal that he did not bother to explain. He had a fine gold moustache growing downwards towards the jaw, and this, with his hollow cheeks and large eyes, bluer even than I had remembered, made him look fragile, aesthetic, in a way I found difficult to reconcile with the big, raw-boned Johnno, all angles and impatience, of four years ago. Europe, it seemed, had deeply transformed him. He sat back now, looking entirely at home, and studied me while he sipped his *grog*.

"You've come with loads of cash, I suppose," was what he said as a result of his scrutiny.

I must have looked surprised. "Not really," I said. "I've got about eighty pounds."

He stared at me, open-mouthed, then groaned, clenched his fist, and beat four or five times on the metal tabletop. "Jesus!" he hissed, and the vowels were ten thousand miles away from good Scots. He ground his jaw. "And I was banking on you to get me out of all this." He jerked his head, indicating Paris: the Boulevard, the black tower of St. Germain des Pres, the cafe tables with their marvellous conversations. "Eighty pounds! How could you do it Dante? It won't last a fortnight."

"It's all I've got," I told him tightly. "When I get to London I'll get a job." I felt hot and angry. After all, I hadn't come all this way to save Johnno from whatever scrapes he had got himself into. What about his six thousand pounds? I had saved my money from the tutoring — which I'd slogged away at for six months at ten and sixpence an hour.

He swung sideways on the elegant metal chair, and sat with his chin on his fist, looking huge and miserable. So this was Paris! Suddenly, turning back he reached across and took my arm. "I'm sorry, Dante. I didn't want to spoil your first night. I was just hoping you'd come with some money, that's all." He tightened his jaw. "This fucking town is a nightmare! If I don't get out soon — I tell you — I'll go right out of my head!"

So instead of carrying him off to London for a long spree on my easy Australian money, I moved into Johnno's shabby little hotel in the Rue Monsieur le Prince.

Walking towards it, along the Boulevard, he warned me against being too easily impressed. Those people in the cafes, for example, the blond Bardot girls and their bearded young men. They weren't French at all. They were Germans, the place was full of them. After two world wars, three violent forcings, the mystic marriage between Europe's masculine and feminine principles was still unconsummated. And these blond shits were trying to do it with TALK! "I don't know what you'll want to look at," Johnno said. "The Musée de l'Homme, the Guimet perhaps — Christian Dior, Père Lachaise. I hope you won't want to see Sainte Chapelle!"

In rather more than a month I saw almost nothing of Paris except what Johnno chose to show me, though I did slip out once or twice, while he was giving his afternoon lesson, to the Jeu de Paumes and on another occasion to the Louvre, where an American in white shorts and sneakers was sprinting up and down the stairs, and in and out of the enormous galleries, to challenge a record.

Johnno preferred to stay in bed till early afternoon reading Chester Himes. Then he wandered round the damp, untidy little room for another hour in his underpants while we decided where to have lunch. Sometimes, when he had no lessons to give, we strolled up to Montmartre and bought sheep's cheese and dates, which we ate in the nearby cemetery, a small classical city with rows and rows of pedimented sentry-boxes — an excellent place, Johnno assured me, for fucking, if you didn't have a room; and the flowers too (he indicated huge pink and white bouquets under rain-dabbled cellophane) were nearly always fresh here, if you got them early in the day. Once we went walking in the woods of Meudon on a silvery afternoon when the birches were just springing into leaf; there were tramps everywhere, with their bundle-shaped women and savage terriers, and we went on to Servres and St. Cloud, where we had coffee on the ruined terrace under the limes; then

116

back to Paris through the Bois. Each night, after dinner at La Source or the student restaurant in the Beaux Arts, we would make our way slowly through the labyrinth of dark alleys behind the Tour St. Jacques ("Mystical" Johnno would proclaim, regarding its proportions in the moonlight), where the tarts stood at regular intervals of two feet or so in the dusky lamplight, heavily made-up à la Bardot and calling to us in their heavily formalized patter. Somewhere in the steamy little cafes behind them were the leather-jacketed toughs who were their pimps, and I think it was the pimp, or at least the knowledge of his presence close by that was the real source of excitement for Johnno. Very often, before deciding to go with a girl, he would ask about her pimp, and we would stand on the pavement with our noses pressed to the grimy glass while she pointed out a cap or a black leather shoulder at one of the tables inside. Johnno would nod approvingly or suddenly call the whole deal off, whispering to me as he slouched away, "No style. Just a jumped-up factory worker." He sang the praises of the pimps with a passionate lyricism that would have done credit to Genet: the elegance of their pointed shoes! and the cars they drove! the way they stood with one hand lightly cupping the crotch, and shifted themselves! the flick-knives hidden away somewhere in the top of a boot! the mean slits of eyes! the way they rolled the spit on their tongue and jetted it in a clean fast gobbet between their teeth!

"It's the mystery of it all," Johnno would whisper, watching one of them entranced, as he moved towards an assignation. "Sperm being transmuted into gold — the apotheosis of capitalism. It's the only

117

place left now where there's any style or anything like a genuine ritual. The mass has become completely debased, did you know that?" He had recently become a Catholic. "They might as well serve it in the supermarket. But this is the real thing. Mystery! Mystery!"

"*Au bord de l'eau,*" he would intone, producing each of the foreign vowels as if he were discovering it for the first time. It was an old phrase for the streets along the river that had been engaged in this busy traffic since the days of St. Geneviève. For Johnno it was a magic incantation.

AU BORD DE L'EAU . . .

One of the girls we met in the Boulevard de Sebastapol became Johnno's mistress — a tiny Algerian called Marfya, who wore black stockings, a grey tweed skirt, and a glossy black motorbike jacket that she shared with her pimp. Johnno went sometimes and hid in her wardrobe when she came back with a client. ("I jerk off," he told me, with a broad, innocent grin.) And once a week or so she came in the early hours of the morning to sleep at Monsieur le Prince and we would have a late breakfast together at the Cafe Danton.

The Rue Monsieur le Prince was a narrow street running diagonally between the boulevards. There was a Vietnamese restaurant that played sad, gonglike music in the evening, a record shop, four or five cheap hotels, and the long wall of the Ecole de Médecine. Although it was less than a hundred yards from the Boulevard with its incessant traffic, it was generally deserted, and unless the police were making one of their periodical raids (which they did every time there was a bomb blast or a murder under the trains at Châtelet), it was as quiet and suburban as the Parc Monceau.

I got used to the raids. Like everyone else I would tumble out of bed at the first sound of the armoured car swinging in over the cobbles, and by the time the first hammering came on the door downstairs would be out on the landing with my passport, while Johnno shouted from the landing below: "Twice in a week, this is! It's driving me crazy. You can see now why I wanted to get out." But when the uniformed officers arrived with their tommy-guns at the ready he was desperately eager not to give trouble. His student permit had expired several months ago, and if they had wanted to the police might have arrested him on the spot. But they were after terrorists, not petty violators of the civil code. They returned Johnno his papers with yet another warning, turned over the bedclothes while one of them covered him with a tommy-gun and the other went through the motions of a quick frisking, and it was over. Then my turn. And the others further up. Generally after a "visitation" Johnno's nerves were too shaken to go back to bed, and after three or four minutes of futile argument I would agree to go out with him and walk until dawn. We would stroll along the silver-grey quays where the tramps slept, stop and have coffee at one of the all-night bars, play the pinball machines whose terrible crash and rattle, in those early hours, had a more violent effect on my nerves than any *flic* with his toylike tommy-gun.

Then I too got my taste of things. Walking quietly

one night in the Place des Vosges, we were suddenly driven into the wall by a screaming armoured car, and in a moment three men had us covered, we were being strong-armed and frisked in a blaze of head-lights, my mouth was bleeding, Johnno lay crumpled up on the path. A week earlier, at Easter, an English girl had been caught in a blast of crossfire on the Pont Neuf, and killed. Now, in the edgy rough-and-tumble of the moment, in the panicky look of the boy who held a gun at my stomach (he couldn't have been more than nineteen, he was red-faced and sweatily ham-fisted) I saw just how it might happen. I had a surge of real fear. With the flush of adrenalin, the realities of the world I had stumbled into, which up till now I had accepted with equanimity — it was so ordinary, the sandbags, the barbed wire had seemed as much a part of Paris as the bookstalls along the quay — suddenly slammed home. What flashed into my head were those moonlit newsreels that had also made up, for a time, my childhood nightmares: people crouching in just this position against just such an iron-spiked wall, while uniformed figures questioned them and dragged them away. It was as if I had suddenly found myself in Europe in the wrong decade — when the Jewish grandmother on my mother's side who had died six years before I was born would have been just enough to make me too a victim of the times. I had broken through into my own consciousness; and Paris — Europe — was a different place.

I also saw now what it was that had happened to Johnno, what it was that was so different about him. His violence was no longer a private disorder. It was part of a whole society's public nightmare. He was free of himself. Cured.

All this time he was full of plans for "getting us out".

"Look," he called excitedly one morning from the bottom of the stair well, "all our problems are solved. We're going to Sweden."

"Sweden?" He was coming up the stairs two at a time. "Isn't Sweden supposed to be the most expensive place in Europe?"

"Yes. That's just the point. We're going to launch you."

I was on my guard, "Oh yes. What as?"

He took a deep breath and went right into his answer before I could interrupt. "As a male tart — because you're dark, you see, and in northern countries where everyone's practically an albino you've got to be dark or you get nowhere. My friend is making all the arrangements. We can hitchhike there in five days or so and take a look at Holland and Belgium on the way: Antwerp, the Rubens House, the Adoration of the Holy Lamb . . . "

"Johnno," I said firmly, "you'd better stop getting all worked up about it. We're not going."

"What do you mean?" He looked hurt.

"I mean," I said, "that without wanting to be a spoil-sport or anything, I'm not interested. If you want to launch someone, launch yourself!"

"But I'm fair!"

"Well, go to Spain then."

He looked uncomprehending. "But f' Christ sake, Dante, in Spain everyone's *poor*!"

I shook my head and went past him down the stairs.

"But I've written to people," he called after me. "Look, I've got a whole list of names — they'll take us straight to the right circles. You won't have to stand around on corners, you know."

"Not me," I said again and kept on walking.

"F' Christ sake!" He plunged the letter into his jacket pocket. "Didn't you ever hear about opportunity knocking only once?" He slouched off, muttering to himself, and slammed his door. He was sulky all evening.

Next day he broached the subject again.

"The Adoration of the Holy Lamb," he began to tell me, "is practically the greatest painting of the entire Middle Ages."

"I don't doubt it," I said shortly, "but the answer is no!"

On the third day, after more sulking, and some heavy hints that what he was now suffering was in some way *my* responsibility, since I had refused, out of selfishness and a terror of real experience that I would obviously never outgrow, to extricate him from this god-awful city — on the third day, he came to terms with things: Sweden was no go. While we were walking round the stone basin in the Luxembourg Gardens, taking advantage of the first spring sunshine, he suddenly stopped, looked at me critically for a moment, took my arm, and said affectionately: "You know, Dante, you were right about that Swedish business. It was silly of me. It would never have worked. You're — well, you're a bit past it, really."

Of course there were other possibilities — as many

122

almost as there were countries. The ultimate was Nepal. Johnno's eyes grew cloudy at the mere mention of it: "You go there," he told me dreamily, "and you're immediately purified."

He sat quiet, still, as if in the rarefied air of the elevation at which he now stood the least exertion might be too much for him. "Pure. Pure!" It was a place he could always shift to, in mind at least, on a few deep inhalations of the hash he got cheap from his Algerian connections. One mouthful took you as far as Beirut. Two more and you were right there in Katmandu.

In the meantime there was the Massif Central, there was Spain. We would take our packs and walk the old Pilgrim Route to Santiago di Compostella, sleeping in the fields now that spring was coming, walking all day, living off the charity of the local peasants. We would look at marvellous Romanesque sculptures, Autun, Souillac.

It was a great plan, and for three or four days Johnno talked of nothing else. He sat hunched over a huge road map spread out on the floor of his room, measuring distances with a school ruler, totting up figures. Names recurred and became yet another of his sacred litanies: Cahors, Sainte Foy de Conques, Vézelay. After the low grey skies of Paris, and trees that were forever dripping, I longed for big breaths of country air and thirty-mile hikes in the sun. But when Johnno saw that I meant it and would set off the moment he gave the word, his enthusiasm cooled and he began to find difficulties. You couldn't live off the charity of the bloody French. They'd let you starve. And Spain was full of policemen. Besides it was too far. Nearly a thousand miles. We'd get there with our legs worn down to the knees. Which was fair enough for *real* pilgrims. We'd better go to Brittany. Or what about Greece?

Johnno had been to Greece two years before with an artist friend from London called Crispin. They had spent five weeks tramping through Crete: beaches, Johnno told me ecstatically, with water so clear you could see your piss in it, and on the Lassithi plateau hundreds of little windmills with triangular white sails, all fluttering in the sun. It was Paradise, and practically the cheapest place in Europe. "The air's so pure," Johnno told me, "you hardly need food at all. A few olives. A little fetta cheese. Once we actually got there, across fucking Jugoslavia, it'd be a dream!"

We didn't go to Greece. Or even to Brittany. Johnno, I soon realized, was mesmerized by Paris, his dreams of leaving it for one corner of Europe or another were simply alternatives that he allowed to exist for a moment because they made Paris itself, and his presence in it, so much more solid and absolute. Paris was the city for which Greece, Spain, Sweden, and other places too numerous to mention, had been rejected. As for me, I was just a tool in Johnno's process of making Paris real for himself, and I soon tired of it.

Greece was the nearest we ever came to an alternative, but it was too difficult to get there. As for the living on air, I heard something of that, and of Johnno's Cretan adventures, when I met Crispin in London during the next winter.

After their first week on the island they had been penniless, and were saved from starvation by the generosity of the Cretan peasants who took them in, fed them on lentils, and allowed them even to sleep in their own matrimonial beds. Johnno, especially, was ravenous to the point of insanity the whole time. They bought a little bag of acid drops each day to stave off the pangs, and agreed to ration them out three at a time. But on the first day, when Johnno had charge of them, all the sweets disappeared after the first distribution. He was contrite. He apologized, grovelled, wrung his hands. He just hadn't been able to help it. He'd been obsessed by the idea of them in his pocket, he'd suffered a complete moral collapse. How could Crispin ever forgive him? He begged Crispin to take charge of the bag himself and see they were shared out properly, as they'd agreed. So all next day, and the day after, Crispin was strict with him. Despite Johnno's pleas to have all his sweets at once, despite his whining, when all three were doled out and swallowed, that he was still hungry, that if he could have another one Crispin could deduct it from tomorrow's lot, Crispin stuck, and Johnno was left to mull over his resentments and sulk. As the day wore on he got more and more abusive. Muttered, ground his teeth. Till Crispin threatened to settle the matter by chucking the whole bloody lot into the sea. Then in the late afternoon, while they were resting in the shade of some olives, Johnno suddenly threw himself on Crispin, overpowered him, snatched the bag of sweets out of his pocket and made off. When Crispin found him at last, under a huge olive tree, deep in the grove, the acid drops were a solid wedge in the corner of his cheek.

So we didn't go to Greece. Instead we went two or three afternoons a week to Johnno's favourite place in Paris, and one, he assured me, of its great sights: the Christian Dior Salon off the Champs Elysée.

"Look at the bitches! Look at their fingernails! Look at their heels!" he'd mutter between his teeth as the cool mannequins, taller than lifesize, painted like totems, paraded up and down the velvet ramps in a room that was all mirrors and strange grottos plastered with shells. They changed with extraordinary rapidity — from Arctic furs, in which only their eyes were visible, to diaphanous rainbow-coloured négligés, all silken swirls and pleats, through which the lines of the body showed up dark against the lights.

"Jesus!" Johnno would hiss.

But after the first half a dozen visits to this glittering shrine, I was bored, and bad-mannered enough to show it. "I suppose," Johnno accused me fiercely, "you'd prefer the Sainte Chapelle. It'd be just like you!"

XII

When the April rains were over at last I crossed to London, which I had always known was *my* destination, and began teaching.

In the first year I shifted school four times, then came to rest at last in a bleak industrial town, all blackened brick, in the north of England, and was gathered into a life as suburban and ordinary in its way as anything I might have settled for at home. In the summers I went to Europe, and got to know one or two towns as well almost as I knew Brisbane — better perhaps since the Brisbane I knew was already changing (my mother's letters kept me informed of old places torn down and of new ones emerging, the Grand Central replaced by a shopping arcade, a whole block in front of the Town Hall ploughed up to make a parking station, the old markets cleared out of the city into a distant suburb, new bridges, new highways); the Brisbane I knew had its existence only in my memory, in the fine roots it had put down in my own emotions, so that a particular street corner would always be there for me in a meeting that had almost changed my life, or in the peculiar fact, half-sweet, half-sad, that it was from there that a certain tram had left, the scene of sentimental adolescent partings. It was the town I would always walk in, in my memory at least, with an assurance I could know nowhere else, finding my way by the smells — a wine-bar, the fruit barrow in a laneway, a hardware shop, the disinfectant they used in Coles. I could have made my way through it blindfold, as I often did in my sleep, amazed to discover that in *my* Brisbane the old markets hadn't been removed at all, and the Grand Central, that extraordinary three-ring circus of my youth, was still in full swing. I could see my own reflections in its mirrors. And Johnno's as well. It would always be there.

Meanwhile, after three years, people at home began to think of me as an expatriate.

An extraordinary denomination. What did it mean? It seemed too grand to fit anything I felt about my position, or any decision I had made to leave Australia and start again elsewhere. I had once found it odd, gratuitous even, that I should be an Australian. I found it even odder, more accidental, that I should be anything else. Friends who came to visit on working holidays were resentful of my being so settled. Their resentment found its object in certain habits that they thought of as non-Australian and therefore a betrayal. Like calling the pictures the "cinema" and sandshoes "plimsols". Like reading *The Times*. Like wearing sandals with socks. Impossible to tell them that all this was quite fortuitous. That I hadn't chosen "silence, exile, cunning", had never left Australia in more than fact. That going to sleep at night was still, for me, to climb high into the glossy dark leaves of the old fig tree outside our kitchen window in Edmondstone Street, with flying-foxes rustling in its darkness, and long golden strands hanging from its branches like a giant's beard, and butcher-birds or mynahs picking about in the sunlight, between roots that pushed in deep under the house, lifting the concrete under the washtubs and even sometimes shifting a stump, far away under our sleep. Expatriate? What did it mean? Nothing it seemed to me. Except that the tree below my bedroom window here was a weeping beech that in summer filled the whole view with its brittle leaves and in winter let through the houses opposite, with frost repointing the edges of their bricks. The children in the flat below hung gobbets of meat from its boughs, and all winter the birds came to peck at strips of belly-pork or pick the last shreds from a mutton chop. A red setter loped through the yellowing stalks of the overgrown garden, sniffing, freezing — hunting blind in his own territory. There was nothing exotic about all this. I taught school all week, drank at the Carnarvon Castle or the Queens on Friday night. Saturday afternoon shopping. A Sunday walk to the top of Bidston Hill, with a long view across open country to an estuary and golflinks by the sea. In the town itself men from the shipyards in their heavy lumbermen's rig and donkey jackets, still grimy from work, dragging their boots over the sawdust in dockside pubs and bursting noisily into the street at closing-time, stumbling off for a piss in cobbled backs. It wasn't something I had chosen. I was here, that's all. I had never left *anywhere* . . .

I heard from Johnno only briefly in those three or four years. Just after Christmas in the first year, he came to London for a wedding: Crispin, who was now the manager of a fashionable gallery, was to

129

marry the niece of a painter, or sculptor, I forget which, and Johnno was best man. Then one summer I had a whole series of postcards from Germany. He and a German boy with the improbable name of Michael Kohlhaas were engaged in a large-scale operation on the autobahn stealing cars (Mercedes for preference), which they drove halfway across the country and disposed of over a cliff. I can't vouch for the truth of any of this, but the cards came at regular intervals over six or seven weeks and from places hundreds of kilometres apart. He was certainly travelling fast, and if the autobahn was not involved I don't know how else he can have been doing it. Or why. His route backwards and forwards across Germany had no fathomable system.

Then silence again: and a long, utterly incomprehensible letter from somewhere in the Bernese Oberland where he was holed up for the winter, "meditating" — the Himalayas being impracticable for the moment, though Switzerland, he assured me, with its tidiness and its obsession with small change, was a poor substitute for Nepal. The realm of the spirit, obviously, had very little to do with either elevation or climate.

Then after another year in which he appeared briefly in Vienna and Bucharest, a jaunty letter from Athens. He was teaching in one of the Berlitz schools at the Pireus. Athens was marvellous. He was utterly happy. Re-generated. Resurrected. I must come and visit him *immediately*.

I didn't go immediately. But I did go at the end of

the next summer.

So there we were again, sitting opposite one another at a white-topped marble table with glasses of Metaxa brandy between us and little sideplates of olives and tomato. The walls were darkly panelled, with old-fashioned advertisements (in English) for fancy biscuits and out-of-date cigarettes. It might have been the Greek Club. Only it wasn't, and neither of us was the same.

After the lean years in Paris Johnno had filled out and was almost plump, as though he had begun to realize in the flesh his own larger possibilities, and was growing to fill them. His hair was longer, his full cheeks clean-shaven, his blue eyes strangely dulled. For the first time since I had known him his exuberance struck me as forced; he might even have been trying, for my sake, to rediscover some idea of himself that he could only fully realize through my presence. He was playing up to my vision of him.

"Dante, Dante! It's so good to see you," he told me for the third or fourth time. "I've been going to pieces in the sun. Look at the belly I've grown." He lifted his loose shirt and showed it. "I've been letting myself go. Greece is so — " He made a vague gesture with his hand, indicating the slack darkish water of the harbour with its small boats rocking above their own shadow, and the stink of fishbones and salt. His eyes glistened and he called the waiter for more drinks. "You'll love it here, Dante, I know you will. So long as you don't expect it to be classical. It isn't you know. It's Byzantine! Soft, dark, utterly corrupt!" He indicated a group of old men slipping beads between their fingers as they looked on at a chess game. Blue-grey smoke drifted across from the pave-

131

ment opposite, where a boy was roasting corn on a charcoal burner, turning and turning the cobs on an open tray and licking his fingers when they burned.

It was to be, for Johnno, the last of Europe. He pointed beyond the harbour wall to where the islands beat east towards Asia: Andros, Naxos, Rodos, Kos — the route Dionysus had come on, stepping from island to island with his message from the heart of the world. "I'll be there in about two years," Johnno said dreamily, as if it was a state you might reach like drunkenness, a journey through time rather than space, across more than the mountain ranges and borders of geography. "There's no hurry. That's one of the things you'll have to learn here: there's no hurry. If it didn't happen yesterday, it will happen tomorrow. Time is — " and he broke off again, with the same indefinable gesture towards the harbour, where the boats rocked on their shadow in no perceptible breeze.

Our days were more leisurely even than in Paris, and Johnno treated my desire to "see things" with mild amusement.

"As if after so long they're going to *disappear*," he'd complain, when I ranged impatiently up and down the room waiting for him to get dressed.

He would lie curled up in a sleeping-bag on the bare floor till well after midday, with the shutters drawn to keep out the sun.

"All right, all *right*!" he'd snap, when I looked in for perhaps the third or fourth time, "just give me time to get on my feet, that's all."

But an hour later he would still be shuffling round the darkened room in his underpants, kicking at the cardboard suitcases that contained his clothes or pausing to read the scraps of paper that were hammered to the wall: messages to himself in his own childish scrawl, pictures and articles from the magazines, a whole page sometimes torn out of a book he was reading, while the book itself joined a dusty pile in the corner, where silverfish nested — abandoned but not thrown away. What clothes were not piled into the three suitcases were either strewn about the floor or hung (clean or dirty I could never tell which) on lines of string that stretched dangerously from the clasp of a shutter to a nail on the wall, then back to another shutter opposite.

"Do be good, Dante. Don't hang about," he'd say, sensing my presence at the open door. "Or make me a coffee. What about that?" He would be peering at a magazine photograph of Ellie Lambetti and rubbing solemnly at his chin. "Then, I promise, Scout's Honour, we'll go to Kaysariani. Only for Christ sake *shit*! I've got to have time to get *up*."

Usually I crept out of the house early, before he had even begun to emerge from the depths of last night's drunkenness, and would see him first in the late afternoon, when he would be brushed and freshened up again for his evening classes.

He had a whole life here that I had no part in. There was an old antique dealer in the Plaka who got him hash in return for favours I was never clear about. I would walk up and down the crowded alleyways, peering into shops full of ikons and patched-up pots or crammed with ironmongery of every sort, ploughs, kettles, anvils, old cauldrons and tripods, chains, motorbike engines — till Johnno reappeared, looking sulky but with his tight little wad of "stuff". He also had a girl in one of the houses at the Pireus, and one day late in my visit he took me down to meet her. We sat about in one of the poky little rooms, laughing, and two of the other girls came in to practise their English, flouncing about in their silk dressing-gowns, giggling, and slipping off whenever there was a call. We had coffee brought in from the cafe opposite by a boy with a shaven head, who came swinging down the street with the five coffees and waterglasses on a silver tray, and while we sipped our coffee, gulped our water, one of the girls tickled him in a corner while the others went off into gales of laughter. He emerged red-faced and angry (he might have been ten or eleven) and clattered about muttering as he gathered up the cups. Johnno went there at the weekend and was away sometimes till Monday night, but the girl never came up to Athens and I saw her only the once. She was a tiny dark girl from one of the islands. Naxos, I think.

Johnno had always liked mysteries. At no time during the past three years had I ever had an address for him — an address, that is, where he was actually living and to be found. In Paris I had written to the Fosse St. Bernard or to the Flore. In Athens he used an address in Monastiraki and I had tracked him down only through the school.

His life here, it seemed to me, was more mysterious than ever. There was an Englishman from the school who came to call for him in his car. Johnno never introduced us, though I frequently opened the door to him, and I suspected somehow that he wasn't from the school at all. If we saw him in one of the city bars, Johnno told me, we must give no sign of recognizing him. He wouldn't want to be seen. And Johnno did translations for a newspaper editor — an

American who had a weekly in Saloniki. He would appear sometimes at a neighbouring table, in a cafe we had just happened to stop in, though it was very much out of our way. Johnno would leave me briefly, talk to the man, sitting close across the table, and we would be off. What was he involved in, I wondered. Drug trafficking? Politics? Of the left? Of the right? It seemed typical of our relationship nowadays that I couldn't tell. It might have been any one of them.

Except for a brief meal in one of the Pireus taverns, which we would eat late in the afternoon, I saw him, for the most part, only at night. I would meet his train at Monastiraki about ten-thirty, after his class. We were free then. To eat at one of the stuffy cavernous restaurants in the Plaka, or at a table on the footpath opposite, talking, reminiscing, bitching, while Johnno consumed tankard after tankard of retsina, till he was so drunk I would have to drag him home and up the narrow stairs to his room. Later, in the early hours towards dawn, I would hear him being violently, wretchedly sick from the lavatory roof. For the first time since I had known him I wondered where he was going, what he was doing with himself. What did he want out of life? What ordinary fate was he in flight from? What would he do next?

"Well," he enquired of me one day, as if to counter a question I had never put, "what will *you* do next?"

I answered without thinking: "I'll go home."

He regarded me scornfully, then nodded. "I always knew you would."

He looked hurt, as if I had betrayed him, then shrugged his shoulders and went back to his drink. He found my decision incomprehensible; but didn't bother to ask why.

I'm not sure I could have told him if he had.

One night late, set off perhaps by the likeness of the little cafe we were drinking in to the Greek Club, and the warmth of the Athenian night to those heavy, subtropical nights in Brisbane when the pavements gave off a heat that rose right up though your shoes, Johnno withdrew a little into some secret place from which he smiled out at me like a mischievous child, then leaning across the marble-topped table began in his old conspiratorial whisper: "Dante, I'm going to tell you something. But it's a secret. I want you to promise you'll keep it."

Worked on by the same uncertain feelings that had inspired Johnno, and glad to see in him some of the old fire, the old mystery, I promised; and he began to tell me.

In that last summer before he left, as a final gesture of defiance, he had gone out each night for a week and set fire to a church: four Methodist, one Congregational, one Anglican, and one of some other nondescript nonconformist creed he had never been sure of. The Catholics had escaped because the bastards always built in stone! No doubt I'd remember the fuss there'd been. A firebug! A maniac! Well, it was *him*. He sat there large and solemn. Bubbling. What did I think of it?

As always with one of Johnno's stories I didn't know what to think. Yes, there had been a firebug. I remembered that well enough. Yes, it would be easy enough to take a can of petrol, crawl under the stumps or through the absurd little gothic window of one of those weatherboard churches in the outer suburbs, which were not much more than one-roomed sheds really, and set it alight. Especially in early summer when dry grass could catch and be ablaze in seconds. Even a bit of broken glass would do that, if the angle was right and the sun high enough. Stony ground, parched half-acre of something like straw with a single hoop-pine or bunya ragged in the wind. I even believed he was capable of it. But whether he had actually *done* it — that was another matter.

"You don't believe me," he said bitterly.

I shrugged my shoulders. "If you say so, yes, I believe you." It didn't sound convincing.

"Well you can check the bloody papers," he said, "*The Courier-Mail*, you'll believe that I suppose. It was in the last weeks of December. I did my last one just before Christmas, at The Gap. I would have done nine altogether to make a cross, but the rain set in and I had to leave one whole arm off. It's all there in the papers in black and white. I don't give a fuck whether you believe it or not."

He looked sulky. Somehow the excitement of it had made him blaze up for a moment like the old Johnno, something impish leaping clear of the heavy body that I had finished off with my failure to respond. I felt mean. As if I had cheated him of some larger dimension of his own improbable existence. Johnno's story was less a confession, I thought, than a rehearsal. I had just rejected one of his finest scenarios.

We did finally make the climb to Kaysariani, on almost my last day in Athens before the long haul across Europe to another London winter.

On the bus out through the hot flat suburbs Johnno was still heavy and bad tempered from last night's drinking. He huddled sulkily in a corner, pulling away savagely when a small child in a woman's arms leaned out and tugged playfully at his hair. But once we were on the slopes of Hymettos, with the last garish villa behind us and the road winding up ahead among dark straight cypress, he relaxed a little and began to point out to me the domes of the churches below, and further off, the pinkish roofs of the Pireus where we went sometimes in the evening to eat souvlakia and drink sweet Samos wine in the smoky taverns. The hillside was a blaze of air, with rows of square metal bee-boxes arranged one above the other in a dazzling terrace and women in black moving slowly across the slope gathering baskets of the wild herbs whose fragrance was everywhere, oregano, rosemary, sage. Far away just under the peak, in a grove darker and thicker than the rest, were the gold crosses of the monastery. When we reached it at last, and stepped through the wall into the chapel forecourt, it was like plunging into a well, it was so cool, so still, the silence was so deep. The darkness of cypress enclosed the place completely. You had to look far up to see the blue of the open sky. Little streams trickled away between green slabs underfoot and seeped between the moss-covered stones of the wall. We drank from a ram's head that uttered a jet of clear, ice-cold water that must have come from the very depths of the mountain.

"There's a spring," I remembered, "a fountain of

Diana or Venus — I read about it in the guide." And I began to take from my duffel the Blue Guide that, to Johnno's disgust, I carried everywhere, like a bloody German!

We examined the frescos in the dome of the chapel, and Johnno declared them rubbishy, poor late-eighteenth-century work, restored, from the look of it, by foot painters. His big loose laugh offended the young monk who had unlocked it for us and I gave him twenty drachmas out of embarrassment. I suggested we look for the spring, which was the source of all those little rivulets whose bubbling filled the court with a sound that I had taken at first for silence. Johnno shrugged his shoulders, and followed me, muttering, up the steep slope beyond the monastery that led, according to my guidebook, directly to the spring. For twenty minutes or more we searched the hillside in the prickly noon heat. Bees droned, grazing on the herbs, and Johnno drove them off with his hat. There were tall dry thistlesticks that caught our trousers, loose stones that slipped underfoot, and everywhere the sound of water, trickling, gurgling, at times it was almost thunderous. But no sign of a spring. Johnno snatched the guidebook from my hand and turned it to left and right, trying to make sense of the map.

"Oh fuck it!" he said at last, flinging the book back to me, "who wants to see it anyway. Let's go down. Do you mind?"

We made our way back down the steep slope, half-crawling, half-sliding, and were about to go back through the gap in the monastery wall when a young woman appeared, fanning herself, the hair sticking sweatily to her brow, with another girl behind her, and then two old women in black.

"You found the spring?" the first girl asked in Greek.

No, we hadn't.

The girl, still blocking our path, turned and shouted down to the older women. They shouted back and forth. Then the girl consulted with the other young woman and they began to climb back through the wall while we slid and scrambled behind.

"You are English?" the girl said, when we were all down. "My cousin and I have learned English very well. My cousin is at work in the Congo for an English company. We would like you," she indicated benches, "to have lunch with us."

The old ladies, who had already settled, lifted their heads in the odd Greek way of agreement, and smiled. They undid bundles which contained rolls with sausage and fetta cheese, tomatoes, olives, cucumber.

"Please," the girl urged, "you are very welcome. A picnic, you see."

We sat and ate on the stone platform under the wall, in the shade of the cypress, while water trickled noisily all about us. We conversed. About the difficulties of English, especially the tenses: present, past, future; past perfect, continuous past, conditional past; conditional, subjunctive — all so difficult because there are no rules! and the young woman from the Congo, who was too deeply aware of the difference between Greek and English habits to be entirely happy about her young cousin's exuberance, told us tersely that she was company secretary to an import-export firm and was in Athens on three months leave. It was cool. The old ladies munched noisily on the tough bread, and the woman from the Congo tore off bite-sized pieces and was still nibbling away long after the rest of us were done. At times when there was nothing to say we smiled.

"Well," the younger one said after a particularly long silence, "it's almost twelve." And she repeated it in Greek to her mother and aunt. Who suddenly went very still.

The girl explained lightly. It was the foolish man in Italy, who had promised the world would end today, with a flood, right now, at twelve o'clock. Hadn't we read it in the papers? He and his foolish people had gone up to a high hill and were waiting there, to be safe. The girl's eyes met mine and she blushed. Well, it was very foolish. Educated people did not believe such things. Of course it was in Italy.

The two old ladies, sitting very still, looked dead ahead. Water gurgled comfortingly. Away in the distance — why hadn't I noticed it before? — was the sound of traffic, and a plane turned to make its run in to the airport. The girl glanced casually at her watch.

"There!" she announced triumphantly. "After twelve o'clock!" She laughed. "Silly! I knew it wouldn't happen."

The two old ladies smiled, shifted on their haunches, smoothed their skirts, laughing.

"Didn't it?"

Johnno had been unusually quiet. Now that he spoke the girl had to turn half about to enquire, puzzled:

"Please?"

"How do you know it didn't? It could have." He gave a sudden violent chortle that startled the old ladies out of their happy calm. "Maybe it did and we

141

didn't notice."

The girl looked distraught. What was he talking about? She couldn't follow. It was the tenses.

"I'm sorry, I have failed to understand," she admitted, deeply disappointed.

Johnno gave another of his harsh belly-laughs and I explained hastily: "A joke. My friend was making a joke."

She smiled weakly and I got up, thanking her, and all of them, the sour cousin, the two old ladies, while Johnno kept mumbling: "How would we know the difference? It'd all go on just the same. How would we know?" I pushed him off down the steps towards the forecourt and on out of sight.

But the notion pleased him. He kept up all day the pretence that it had happened after all.

"How do you feel, Dante? Can you feel the difference?" He poked himself in the tyre of fat around his ribs. "I feel exactly the same. It's marvellous. Should we eat do you think? Look at that old lady eating baklava, she hasn't even realised. Look at the way she's licking the back of her fingers. It all looks exactly the same. Exactly! Not a scrap of difference. Maybe it happened ages ago. Ages! How would we know? How would we ever know?" He stopped and shook his head, amazed, in front of an old man selling lottery tickets, with row upon row of papers stuck into slots at the top of a pole like a Sioux war lance. It kept him light and happy till well after dinner.

Which we did eat after all, at a little pavement cafe in the Plaka, while cats prowled the stones beyond an iron railing — the last remains (unnecessary to visit, according to my Blue Guide) of Hadrian's library. *Sic transit gloria mundi . . .*

XIII

Back in Brisbane just after Christmas, I discovered that I had made a terrible mistake.

There was a girl I had met in England who was more than half the reason for my return, but suddenly everything that had seemed possible while we were still footloose in another country, with all the ease and openness that comes from having only such possessions as will fill a rucksack and a couple of light cases, now disappeared under difficult considerations like where we might live (she came from Grafton and was excessively devoted to her parents), the sort of "home" we might settle for, and whether the wedding, since there must after all be a wedding, should take place here or there, in church or out of it. Nothing seemed to me to be open or free any more. It was to be decisions at every point, a whole set of little locks into a life I had never cared for, and doubted, even now, if I could accept.

We saw one another at weekends (I went down on the overnight train), and in between had expensive long-distance quarrels on the telephone. I spent my time mooning about the house waiting for her to call or waiting impatiently till I could call her. We broke off, made up again, broke. The thing was hopeless but wouldn't end. My parents, who thought I had come back to get a job and settle, were bitterly disappointed. From their point of view I was exactly where I had been four years ago, and there were times when I felt so too. Brisbane, where I sometimes thought of myself as having "grown up", was a place where I seemed never to have changed. Just turning a corner sometimes on a familiar view, or a familiar sign: *Fullars Dry Cleaning, Red Comb House Ind. Coop.*, made me step back years and become the fourteen-year-old, or worse still, the twenty-year-old I once was, helpless before emotions I thought I had outgrown but had merely repressed. All my assurance, all my sophistication about foreign places and performances and food, like the growing heaviness round the shoulders, was a disguise that might fool others but could never fool me. Elsewhere I might pass for a serious adult. Here, I knew, I would always be an aging child. I might grow old in Brisbane but I would never grow up.

And there were other ghosts as well. Even more disturbing. The ghosts of school boys still visible behind the solid, dull presence of friends I ran into in Queen Street or met at Hamilton when I went to watch my nephews tussle on a rugby field (fierce, dodgy seven-year-olds), and found half the fathers in the crowd were my contemporaries: lawyers, stock-brokers with seats on the Exchange, architects, accountants, successful real-estate agents, all thickening out of whatever grace I had remembered in them but retaining, for all their ponderous self-assurance, some hint of boyishness that seemed like a national trait, though all their fire had been delegated to those small muddy figures on the oval, breaking out of the mob with a ball or dodging skilfully downfield towards the touchline. I went and had drinks with one of them (we had nothing to say to one another) while half a football team tumbled about in the back of a station-wagon, and visited others at home. They seemed oddly apologetic at being caught out like this, running to fat from too little exercise and too much beer, inclined to boast about how quickly they had made it, uneasily proprietorial as they allowed the children to show off a little and their wives to be admired. I recognized the elements of success. Scrubbed colonial furniture, the pennants for swimming and football in the children's rumpus room, a Blackman lithograph. I could appreciate also the technical expertise, a hard competence at whatever it was they did that had taken them easily to the top.

But it depressed and saddened me, and was half the reason, perhaps, for my difficulties with the Grafton girl. I grew increasingly restless and ill at ease. Just to be out of the house a little I took to reading again at the Public Library, and was on my way there one steamy, drizzly afternoon when I was astonished to see making towards me along Queen Street two more ghosts — the most unexpected of all: Johnno, huge, spade-bearded, wearing an olive-green safari jacket, shorts, desert boots; and dancing along a few steps behind him a spring-haired figure, skinny as a rake, whom I recognized immediately as the Mango.

Johnno looked put out, as if I had discovered him in a deception. Yes, yes, he had been in Australia for three months. Didn't I know? — there was a mineral boom. He was working on an oil survey, out on the Condamine, making over a hundred pounds a week. It was crazy. He couldn't stop now because he and the Mango (yes, of course, I remembered the Mango) were on their way back after a weekend break. He'd drop me a line and maybe next time he was down we could have a drink together.

He was enormous. Larger than life. Perhaps three stone heavier than he had been in Greece. And bore an uncanny resemblance, I thought, to one of his old heroes, Ubu Roi. Gross, dishevelled, his flesh flabby and yellow behind the miner's beard. Coarsened but un-tanned by the sun.

I walked them to the station. We stopped twice, once at the British Empire, once at the Windsor, while Johnno swallowed a slug of gin, pouring it straight down his throat; and by the time the train left he was relaxed again and seemed pleased to see me. We really would meet. Maybe even next week-end. We'd go to some of the old places or to Stradbroke Island. I'd hear from him on Thursday.

I didn't hear from him for over a month. Then one Friday night, as in the old days, there was a phone call. He was at the Royal George in the Valley. Why didn't I come in and meet him?

I arrived late and found him drinking with two fellow-workers from the survey, a Swede whose name I didn't catch and a pale, freckled man in khaki shorts and singlet who was called "Blue". They were driving back next day in the Swede's car, and there was a good deal of discussion about when they would set out. Finally it was settled, we shook hands all round and Johnno and I left. Johnno was in one of his moods. His hand was bandaged, an accident he told me with a primus stove. He seemed preoccupied. A couple of drinks more made him maudlin, then abusive, then simply weary, and though we tried hard enough, the evening failed to catch fire.

If Johnno had intended us somehow to revive the exploits of our youth, Brisbane itself had taken measures to prevent us. The Greek Club had been moved back a street towards the Gardens, and we took a good twenty minutes to convince ourselves that we weren't dreaming when it refused to reveal itself in the old place. The new club had an open courtyard and a regular restaurant and looked eminently respectable. The brothels too were gone — closed by the new government as part of a campaign to destroy the city's reputation as a tropical backwater, sluggish, colonial, degenerate, and force it into the present. The menagerie in the Gardens had been removed at the same time, and the unfortunate animals, a few scrawny monkeys, a demented ape, some moth-eaten wallabies, and several cages of parakeets and lovebirds, had been carted off and exterminated. Their cages were burned and the gardens reorganized to make pretty walks, with lily ponds and a cascade. There was no report on the inmates of the two houses. But the houses themselves were still there behind their corrugated-iron walls. Nobody had bothered to burn them.

It was the same all over. The sprawling weatherboard city we had grown up in was being torn down at last to make way for something grander and more solid. Old pubs like the Treasury, with their wooden verandahs hung with ferns, were unrecognizable now behind glazed brick facades. Whole blocks in the inner city had been excavated to make carparks, and there would eventually be open concrete squares filled with potted palms, where people could sit

147

about in Brisbane's blazing sun. Even Victoria Bridge was doomed. There were plans for a new bridge fifty yards upstream, and the old blue-grey metal structure was closed to heavy traffic, publicly unsafe. There would eventually be freeways along both banks of the river that would remove forever the sweetish stench of the mangroves that festered here, putting their roots down in the mud; the old boathouse where we had gone to dances was burnt-out and the pontoon where Johnno had swum that night during the flood had been dismantled and taken for scrap. Huge pieces of earth-moving equipment and cranes with iron-jawed buckets and hooks presided in the moonlight over dirt piles that seemed more extensive in some parts of the town than what was still standing.

It is a sobering thing, at just thirty, to have outlived the landmarks of your youth. And to have them go, not in some violent cataclysm, an act of God, or under the fury of bombardment, but in the quiet way of our generation: by council ordinance and by-law; through shady land deals; in the name of order, and progress, and in contempt (or is it small-town embarrassment?) of all that is untidy and shabbily individual. Brisbane was on the way to becoming a minor metropolis. In ten years it would look impressively like everywhere else. The thought must have depressed Johnno even more than it did me. There wasn't enough of the old Brisbane for him to hate even, let alone destroy. The others had got in before him.

I never did discover why he had come back.

What had happened to Nepal? Was it really Miles he had been heading for all these years? What sort of defeat of his expectations, what moment of panic, had brought him back full-circle, the long way round from Brisbane to the Condamine, via the Congo, Paris, London, Hamburg, Athens? He was too drunk to give me any coherent answer — or pretended to be — and all I could make out of his mutterings was our need to "destroy the myth". *He* had destroyed the myth two nights ago. With Bill Mahoney. Bill knew what it was all about. He kept repeating this, with great loose guffaws, and moments between of looking baffled and stricken. Then submerged into silence, sodden and morose. I found no way of reaching him. At last when he dozed off, I went out, called a taxi, and sent him home.

Somewhere during all this he had invited me up to the camp for the weekend. But I didn't dare leave the Grafton business for that long and put him off. Sometime later, I told him, when it was cooler. He shrugged his shoulders. It was up to me.

About eleven next morning he called. He sounded clear-headed, almost his old self — somehow I found it easier to accommodate myself to Johnno's voice, which had changed so little over all these years, than to the lumbering presence I had wrestled with last night. He was ringing to tell me that he hadn't gone with the Swede after all. He was going back later by plane. He told me this three or four times, without explanation. Then hung up. The message seemed to me to have no particular importance, and I didn't think of it again till over a week later. Then circumstances made me go back to Monday's paper and look carefully at an item I had barely noticed when it first

149

appeared — one of the weekend's many road accidents. A Holden with two men in it had plunged over the Range below Toowoomba late on Sunday morning, and the occupants had been killed outright. One, the owner of the car, was a Swedish migrant aged thirty-three, from Taroom; the other was a labourer of no fixed address. They had been working at an oil-drilling site in the South West.

There was no doubt in my mind that they were the two men I had met at the Royal George, and I thought also of something Johnno had said to me more than once over the years: that half the road accidents that were reported in the papers weren't accidents at all, but carefully managed suicides.

Is that what he had intended? Is that what he and the Swede and the man called Blue had been planning at the Royal George before I arrived? I couldn't believe it. Yet what else would explain Johnno's phone call and his insistence that he hadn't gone?

For by then Johnno's own death had been reported, in a five-line paragraph in *The Courier-Mail* (which had got him after all): *Accidental drowning near Miles*. It had happened on Saturday, less than a week after the car crash. He had been pulled out of the water by a fellow worker, Doug Wilson (the Mango), who had tried without success to resuscitate him. There would be an inquest.

The Mango!

One of those shadows Johnno had tried so hard to lose all those years back, he had reappeared just two months ago to be in at the end, someone who just happened to be there, sleeping off a drinking bout at the edge of the weir, when Johnno dived in and failed to come out again. It was the Mango, a skinny nine-stoner, who had dragged his huge water-logged body up out of the weeds and pumped away, as we were taught to do in the Junior Lifesaving Team at school, till he himself collapsed with exhaustion.

And of all the rivers in the world that might have risen up to take him, it was the Condamine, whose course we had drawn in so often on our homework maps of Queensland and its river systems — the Condamine that we had represented, like all our rivers, with a blue line of solid ink, but which was, we knew, only the ghost of a river for two seasons of the year, a few glittering waterholes in a channel of ridged white sand, flowing furtively underground. In one of its more abundant moments it had reappeared to swallow him.

The Mango and the Condamine! Who could have foretold it on any one of those afternoons, years back, when all three of them might already have been in some sort of conjunction? — the Mango leaning over Johnno's shoulder during Mr. Campbell's geography lesson to "copy", while Johnno traced in the fictitious course of the stream, from its rise in the MacPherson Ranges, about a hundred miles southwest of where we were sitting, to where, far away in the inland, it crossed the border, joined the Murray-Darling system, and made its slow way, by other names, to the Bight. The pattern might have been there already if we had had eyes to see it. Now at last it was clear. Or was it? The pattern had been achieved.

I thought of Johnno's promise, that in seven years every last particle of Australia would be squeezed out of him, he would have freed himself of the whole monstrous continent.

Well, the seven years were up. Like a bad charm. And it was Johnno who was gone. Australia was still there, more loud-mouthed, prosperous, intractable than ever. Far from being destroyed, the Myth was booming. There were suggestions that it would soon be supporting thirty million souls. Australia was the biggest success-story of them all. Real estate was pushing deeper into the gullies, higher towards the crest of every visible hill. New fast highways ribboned across country, with service stations all steel-and-glass, motels all glass-and-polished-wood, identical from Cairns to Albany. At the city's edge, the dumpyards were now receiving not only the cars we had learned to recognize and covet on our way home from school, the Vanguards and Austin Atlantics of 1948, but the newer streamlined jobs on whose back seats we had fumbled and flared: the Ford Customlines and Minis of the late fifties — all indistinguishable scrap. In the old city centres slim tower-blocks were staggering towards the moon like grounded rockets aimed at nowhere, vying perhaps with the figures, forever climbing, of the Stock Exchange, where oil and mineral stocks were reaching astronomical heights, an index of Australia's extra-ordinary confidence in its own future — in the black sea of oil sleeping untapped under impossible deserts, that inland sea, invisible to the eye, that the last century had dreamed of and never discovered. It was *there* at last. Even Johnno had come to believe in it.

I turned again and again to that paragraph in the paper.

"So — you don't believe me. *The Courier-Mail* now, I suppose you'd believe *that*!"

He too had submitted himself at last to the world of incontrovertible event. Johnno was dead. *The Courier* said so. It must be so.

I was still reading and re-reading that brief paragraph when the postman arrived.

There, on the top of the pile, was a letter in Johnno's big scrawling hand. I read it quickly, then screwed it up, tossed it across the room, redeemed it, read it slowly again. Its tone was that of every letter or postcard I had ever received from him. His cards from Rosebery and Mount Isa. From the Congo. From Paris. "One of my native boys will walk all night to deliver this," he had once written me from his camp on the borders of Rhodesia. "And you won't even bother to reply. He's worth a dozen of you." It was true. I always owed him an answer. There was always someone else I cared for more.

I thought disquietingly of moments when the whole course of events as they stood between us quivered expectantly, and might have gone another way: an afternoon whose heat now returned so powerfully to my imagination that sweat started out all over my skin — when I had gone to Johnno's place with my first stolen goods, two screwdrivers and a matchbox jeep that I had meant to present to him as some sort of offering. Remembering how all afternoon the occasion had refused to declare itself. Something the over-warm day had been expected to produce failed to eventuate, since I had located its excitement in *my* secret, in my three foolish prizes; and when I brought them out the occasion was defused, Johnno had been cheated of some revelation of his own. I thought now, painfully, of his tolerant amusement and my own naivety. And years later, in

Athens, when I was struggling to get him home one night and we had come to rest for a moment in a dirty shopfront, his whole drunken weight against me, he had laughed suddenly, his mouth close to my ear, and said: "You know Dante, when we were at school, I used to think of you as the most *exotic* creature — so strange and untouchable. Like a foreign prince." My mind had whirled, a whole past turning itself upside down, inside out, to reveal possibilities I could never myself have imagined. He gave a harsh laugh. Was the joke on him or on me?

His last letter had neither address nor date. It was scrawled across a page torn out of a company ledger:

Dante,

Please please come. Or we could go to Stradbroke for the weekend. Why don't you ever listen to what I say to you? I've spent years writing letters to you and you never answer, even when you write back. I've loved you — and you've never given a fuck for me, except as a character in one of your funny stories. Now for Christ sake write to me! Answer me you bastard! And please come.

love
Johnno

XIV

The service was at ten thirty on the Wednesday morning. I took a bus marked "Crematorium" from under the fig tree in King George Square, and in the mid-morning dazzle we sped out through the city, past suburban schools where kids were lining up in the playground, or being marched in to a fife band; past sagging verandahs where two symmetrical palms stood on either side of a red-stained path, or allotments where women with huge washing baskets staggered to a clothes hoist standing solitary in a yard; past roadworks where men in shorts and muddy boots were boiling a billy for morning tea. Then off the highway into a dry, treeless gully, till the crematorium appeared high up on a slope: a parapet of variegated stone; dark verticals of pine; then as we swung into the courtyard, a glimpse, beyond classical arcades, of a chimney stack.

The chapel was unnaturally cool, its white walls pierced by stained-glass gothic lights, where angels of a geometrical variety, vivid, sexless, undenominational, broke the harsh sunbeams into eddies of scarlet and mauve. Music was being piped in. It arrived, like the coolness, through holes in the floor — bubbling up softly between the basalt flags. There were altar rails of superbly polished brass, but no altar. Just a tilt where the coffin rested, end on and slightly elevated towards us. On either side a jar of arum lilies, naked and white.

The bus had come in early. The chapel, empty at first, except for his mother in the front row, supported by aunts and a large uncomfortable uncle, began to be crowded, as newcomers shuffled into the narrow pews, their feet scraping on the flags, their whispered apologies clearly audible as they jostled down a row. I felt someone slide into the seat behind me.

"I had no idea you were back even," she whispered.

It was Binkie, in a black suit, with a little pillbox hat.

"Isn't it awful!" She looked suddenly alarmed at the loudness of her own voice in the quiet. "I only came," she breathed, "because I saw it in the paper."

The eulogy was delivered by a Church of England clergyman who was a friend of the family. He hadn't had the honour of knowing Johnno himself, but he did know Johnno's mother, who was a fine woman, and several of his uncles, and felt therefore that he could say something of this young man who had been snatched away — I'm not certain now, but I think he did say "in the flower of his youth". I thought of all those Anzac services I had attended at school, when the honour-boards were read aloud round the Hall and the names intoned in what seemed then to be an endless litany. The war-dead were only too familiar, the first and second sons of families whose names appeared on warehouses and wharves around the city, on timber mills, factories, department stores, and whose big tumbledown houses I had known in my childhood, ramshackle mansions going to ruin in the charge of two old-maid sisters whom we ran messages for, or as they got dottier and dottier, laughed at in their floppy lace hats. The dead had the same names as our neighbours, or boys in the class above us. They were sixth-formers who had never grown old and simple-minded like their sisters. And just reading off the places where they fell, Ypres, Mons, Gallipoli, Pozièrs, Bullecourt, evoked a peculiar atmosphere of golden splendour and colonial chivalry that we might have longed for like a broken dream. Their deaths were both tragedy and fulfillment. They were noble, dedicated, remote, and too good for the rest of us in our prickly flannels, bored with the rhetoric that made this other, earlier generation sound oddly as if they had never stood where we now stood, had never faked a geometry exercise or cribbed a Latin unseen, scribbled dirty words on lavatory walls, had evil thoughts, existed in the flesh that so palpably contained us. Johnno had been in those days the most irreverent of us all. Making jokes out of the corner of his mouth about some of the names as they were read, finding double-entendres in the speeches of the tedious old heroes who came back from the dead to address us. What the minister was doing now was forcing *him* into that splendid company. Johnno too was to be a golden youth cut off in the fullness of his promise. I realized with a shock, as I considered the faces here, their seriousness, their response to what the minister was creating out of Johnno's ribald, heavy-in-the-flesh reality, what dying really means. It means no longer to exist in the minds of the living as a real presence, intractably solid and unique, but to suffer metamorphosis into a pale, angelic figure in whose company we would never raise our voice or

157

giggle or take off our clothes; an insubstantial abstract of such empty recommendations as "devoted son", "loyal friend", "a splendid example to us all".

The clergyman had finished. He folded his hands and turned forty-five degrees towards the coffin, in deferential expectation. After a moment's pause that was filled with a tasteful swelling of music, a little panel slid open in the wall, the coffin rose miraculously on its tilt, and Johnno moved slowly away from us. There was nothing to be shocked at. Music spiralled up, the coffin's pace was dignified but swift, the little panel in the wall closed again, slowly, soundlessly, and it was over. We shuffled out into a solid wall of sunlight. After the coolness of the chapel it was like the edge of an axe.

Binkie walked with me to the parapet. We didn't speak. Johnno's mother had come down the steps into the courtyard and was accepting the handshakes of the other mourners. Under the Roman columns of the arcade a group was gathering for the next service, and I could see the bus making its way zig-zag up the valley, its metal flashing as it turned between the hills.

"We'd better speak to Johnno's mother," I said.

Binkie looked bewildered. "Oh — it's no good me going, Dante. She wouldn't even know who I am. I'll — just wait for you in the car." She made a vague gesture towards the carpark at the end of the terrace. "It's a Holden station-wagon. Blue."

I waited till the last of the mourners had left.

"Dante!" Johnno's mother exclaimed when I approached at last. "Oh Dante!" She clutched my arm and nodded speechlessly. Then after a moment recovered and said: "You haven't changed a bit. You look — exactly the same — "

She looked at me hard, thinking of Johnno perhaps; and I realized suddenly how she must hardly have known him when he reappeared at last after all those years, can hardly have believed that the fair, coltish boy who had gone off and remained just like that in her memory, had grown huge and sodden, every stone a proof of how far he had out-grown her knowledge of him, how far he had moved away. Her gaze flickered and she put her hand to her mouth.

"But I'm not sad," she insisted when she had recovered a little. "I refuse to be sad. He's happy. I know he is! He's with Nietzsche and Schopenhauer. You must come and see me, Dante. There's a book with addresses in it. He had friends all over you know — Paris, London, Athens. I want to write and tell them — what's — happened to him . . . "

She covered her mouth again, and a woman in a straw hat, who might have been a sister-in-law, took her arm and made a little sign to me to leave. I hurried towards Binkie's car. Thinking what some of those "friends" of Johnno's (girls whose address he had been given, a dealer who could get him hash) would make of a letter announcing that Edward Athol Johnson was dead, drowned, in Australia. Lifting their shoulders in puzzlement.

Binkie drove without speaking, hunched forward over the wheel and frowning against the glare. She had slipped her shoes off and was wearing beaded driving-slippers. The hat had been tossed carelessly onto the back seat.

"It must be seven years," she said at last. And her eyes flicked sideways to examine me a moment, then away. "You haven't changed a scrap, you know that,

Dante?" She smiled, and put her hand affectionately on my knee. "I've changed like hell! — Oh, there's no need to pretend I haven't. Did you know I've got two kids? I've settled down, just the way they said I would. It's not so bad."

She smiled again. She was plumper than she used to be, had more freckles. The skin had begun to break up round her eyes, and thicken, in a way that I thought of as Irish. What hadn't changed was her voice. Low and dark like warm molasses. The rum-and-Coke girl.

"Do you think he did it deliberately?" she asked after a little silence.

I didn't know. He could have. I just didn't know.

Binkie shook her head, peering hard ahead at the intersection, where we were about to join the main stream of traffic into town.

"I never understood him, not from the beginning, never at all," she said. "I used to think about him a lot after he went. I was crazy about some of the boys I knew, and now I can hardly even remember their names. Isn't that awful?" She gave one of her bubbly little laughs. "But Johnno was —" She shook her head again, and whatever it was she was going to say went underground, into silence, while she watched a red light up ahead tick slowly towards green. Suddenly as she changed gears and moved forward: "Did you ever read *A Hero of our Time*, Dante? He gave it to me once and I picked it up — oh, just a few months ago and read it for the first time. I suppose he was trying to make me see something in it. About him, I mean. But I still don't know what." She gave me a sharp look, as if her mind had moved off quickly elsewhere. "Are you going to stay this time Dante, or will you

160

go again?"

"Yes," I said, "I'm going to stay," — and realized immediately that it was a decision I hadn't known was made.

She dropped me in the Valley and I promised to ring.

"Please do, Dante," she said, holding my hand through the window. Tears began to shine in her eyes and she made a little gesture of impatience with herself and shoved the car savagely into gear. "I wish I understood things," she said, half to herself. "I've always been so bloody dumb!" She laughed. "They always told me that too." She put her foot down and trailed her hand from the window in a last wave.

That wasn't quite the last of it. Two nights later I had a phone call. It was Johnno's friend Bill Mahoney. He had recognized me at the funeral and wondered, after all this time, if we mightn't meet. He was an intern at the Mater Hospital. Maybe we could have drinks together on Saturday morning.

Bill Mahoney! The exterminating angel! The young Nachaev!

The Criterion at eleven o'clock on Saturday morning was almost empty, the long marble bar had no more than a dozen drinkers, there were two more at tables in the gallery, and I had no difficulty in recognizing one of them as Bill. A plump impressive-looking man who might have been forty, round-faced and bald as a baby, he was raising his hand to catch my eye.

"I think we were supposed to meet," he said,

coming down the two marble steps. He began to
stutter. "I-I-I'll get you a drink." He motioned me to
a table under the stained-glass window at the rails of
the gallery and went on down to the bar. Rebel, spy,
terrorist, I told myself. And was surprised by his
mildness (though of course I oughtn't to have been)
and by his babylike softness, that was due, perhaps,
to nothing more than the limpness of the damp, hairy
hand he had offered me and the glow of fuzz around
his skull.

"Johnno told me a good deal about you," he said
when we were both settled and had had time to
regard one another for a moment over the tops of our
glasses. His mouth dimpled. "I-I was rather scared of
you," he admitted. "You're n-n-not what I
expected."

"*You* were scared?"

He looked up quickly, and I think we both realized
at the same moment what Johnno's game had been,
and felt guilty, sitting here, of the same disloyalty.
We were survivors of a sort, Bill and I. Mildly sipping
our beer on a warm Saturday morning. Slightly
shame-faced. With nothing between us but our unfinished drinks, and the shadow in each of our
thoughts of the picture Johnno had created for us,
out of impatience, perhaps, with the reality. Spy,
terrorist, our very own Rimbaud. Is that how Bill had
thought of me?

He took out a pipe and began to fill it from a
leather pouch. He had seen a good deal of Johnno,
one way and another, over the last couple of months.
He'd been up to the camp and they'd swum at the
very place where it happened: a pool below the weir,
where the river widened under a screen of basket

willows. The local school kids had rigged up swinging ropes and a plank for diving. It was all perfectly safe. A suburban swimming pool. No rocks, no snags, no currents.

"So what happened then?"

Bill pushed tobacco down with his thumb, took out his matches, pushed again, lit a match, and got the thing alight and smoking. His slowness, I thought, was a form of protection. Against what? The stutter? Or was there after all something in him that his silence, his caution, was keeping at bay? He was too subdued.

"An accident," he said at last, frowning. And then, with another appearance of the dimple at the corners of his mouth, "Whatever that means."

"You're satisfied it was an accident?"

He stared ahead as if he hadn't heard my question. Sucking at the pipe. "Of course," he said after what seemed an age, "it's what the inquest *decided*. I was there, I gave evidence. An open and shut case. It's also, incidentally, where the medical evidence points. So there you are."

He looked at me, smiling, and I suspected him, ungenerously perhaps, of playing with me.

"And that's all?"

"N-no, it's not all. It was also an accident that couldn't have happened. Impossible, in that particular place."

So there we were again.

As for the night before my meeting with Johnno, when they had, as Johnno had put it, "destroyed the myth", there was nothing to tell. Or nothing he would tell. Johnno had been pretty drunk. But then he was always pretty drunk these days. They had

picked up a couple of girls and driven out to a crossing to swim. There was an argument, Johnno had hit
one of the girls, Bill had some trouble calming her
down — the usual thing. They'd dropped the girls off
in the Valley and he'd driven Johnno home. He'd had
some harebrained scheme about their burning a
church down, and had spent most of the journey
going through the details of how they'd do it —
getting the petrol from Barnes Auto, in a drum,
finding a likely place, some little weatherboard out in
the sticks, lighting it up from underneath . . .

"You know how he could get himself worked up."
Bill looked at me with his innocuous smile.

"And that was all?"

I remembered Johnno's bandaged hand and his
story about the primus stove.

"It's all I *know*," Bill said, firmly.

And in the end, perhaps, it doesn't matter. A
suicide with some of the shocking randomness of
accident — an accident so aesthetically apt as to have
all the elements of a humorous choice. Johnno's
death would have to confound us. It would have to
be a mystery, and of his own making. It would have
also to defy the powers of medicine and the law to
establish their narrow certainties. It would need to be
explicable, at last, only as some crooked version of
art.

For what else was his life aiming at but some
dimension in which the hundred possibilities a situa-
ation contains may be more significant than the
occurrence of any one of them, and metaphor truer

in the long run than mere fact. How many alternative fates, I asked myself, lurking there under the surface of things, is a man's life as we know it intended to violate?

Epilogue

Among the last of my father's belongings to be cleared away were the only two books I had ever seen him consult, the only books, I believe, that he ever owned.

One was a big old-fashioned ledger, the sort of ledger — imitation leather boards, marbled end-papers — that a young man of ambition might acquire to record three decades of prospective credits and debits, the day by day progress of a phenomenal career. It was empty, save for a curious chart that had been traced on tissue and pasted neatly between the leaves. All jagged peaks dipping sharply towards plateaux, and then deeper still into level valleys and troughs, it looked like the Himalayas in cross-section, or one of the voice-charts we used to make in the language laboratory by shouting nonsense into a tube. It was in fact, as my father had often explained, a graph of the boom years and the years of depression between 1913 when he acquired it and 1994.

My father believed in this sheet of flimsy, yellowing paper as he believed in the Holy Ghost. The neatly ruled lines and small, perfectly formed figures were in his own hand, and every deal he had ever made, every property he had ever bought or sold, every turning his life had taken in the world of public triumphs and disasters, was charted there on its peaks and lows. It was the record, crudely projected, of his life, and at the same time the map of an era. I had spent long hours of my childhood poring over it, fitting my own birth date to one of its most insistent lows and asking the oracle what the world would be like when I was twenty-one, twenty-nine, thirty. It wouldn't matter much after that. Turning back to the old chart now I felt as close as I ever would feel to the forces that had guided my father's life and given it shape. That line on the page was what he had tuned his soul to, taking, as the graph did, the shocks of history.

The other book, which was wide and flat with a royal blue cover, had been one of the most treasured objects of my childhood. It was called *A Young Man with an Oil-Can*, and it celebrated the genius of a young Scot, James MacRobertson, who, beginning with just an oil-can (which appeared on the frontispiece and was a little like the boiler in which Mrs. Allen did our wash), had gone on to found the biggest chocolate factory in the Commonwealth. The factory building, many-windowed and square, loomed up in double exposure — a solid future already branded with his name, Pty. Ltd. — behind a snapshot of James MacRobertson himself, a wide-mouthed young man with shoulder-length black hair, who stood with his sleeves rolled up beside a can in which he was boiling, perhaps, his first sticky confection. I thought this effect quite magical, and only less impressive in my young experience than the colourplates which followed. They, of course, were incomparable, and seemed as beautiful to me then as anything I had ever seen or could imagine, a sort of colonial Book of Hours.

They represented the full range of the MacRobertson products: Columbines, Cherry Ripe, Old Gold, etc., and you got your first glimpse of them through a layer of the finest tissue — it was like peering through the frosted glass of a sweetshop window. Lift the tissue, take a deep breath, and there they were. A jar of boiled lollies, glistening pink and yellow, and in every conceivable shape: scallop-shells, ovals, little barber-pole cylinders with pinched ends, medallions with roses in their depths, even some bite-sized candy-striped pillows that smelled (I could actually smell them) of a medicinal spice like the ambulance tent at Scarborough. Most evocative of all, since it spoke so directly of solid riches, was the MacRobertson Special Old Gold Selection that we bought for my mother's birthdays; with dubloons, ropes of pearl and other precious stones spilling from a pirate's chest, and beside it, the open gold box with its own pile of treasure, the delicious hard and soft centres in their jewel-like wraps.

It was a book, I suppose, that my father turned to as other men in other places have turned to Homer or the *Pilgrim's Progress*, the palpable record of a great national mythology. You began like James MacRobertson with an oil-can and you ended up with a book like this. Or you started like T. C. Beirne and James McWhirter with rival barrows on opposite sides of a street and you ended up with the huge department stores, one firmly Catholic, the other staunchly Protestant, that faced one another across Brunswick Street in the Valley. Success of the golden sort is possible to anyone with the energy and vision to go out for it — that was what the Young Man with the Oil-Can taught; and my father, at least, believed it.

His oil-can had been a horse and dray. His equivalent to James MacRobertson's factory was our heavy, over-furnished house in Arran Avenue and my mother's collection of Venetian glass, Dresden figurines, Noritaki, a whole teaset of which she had miraculously saved (while the rest of Brisbane were smashing their Japanese dinner-plates) on the grounds that it was a wedding present from her favourite brother — a twenty-one piece gilded white lie. This was life as it is lived on the peaks of the famous graph, a real success story. But then, any story that matters here is a success story. The others are just literature.

Still, those troughs at the bottom of the graph are also part of the story. The most impressive fact of my early childhood was the Depression. I can remember the men, worn, shy-looking men in felt hats and threadbare waistcoats, who came to our door for work, misled perhaps by our huge, over-grown garden, and were given food at the bottom of the stairs. There were swaggies on the road and under the trees in Musgrave Park. Like other children in those days we were warned to keep away from them. Otherwise we might disappear and be discovered headless one morning in a dirty sack. When, later in the decade, they themselves disappeared, it was I suppose into the A. I. F. There were boom years then, and 1942, when we were all in imminent danger of destruction, is one of the dizziest peaks on my father's graph. But even then there were old-timers, like Peg-leg, who had not been drafted into prosperity and still came hat in hand for something to help him through the week. My father had a dozen old mates like Peg-leg, who had fallen on hard times, or had never fallen on good ones. Some of them he knew from his fighting days, they were old fans. Others from the early years when he had carried from the markets. He never failed to stop when they hailed him, and never refused the few bob that they would immediately, my mother assured us, drink away in one of the Valley wineshops, whose panelled half-doors only the "lowest" ever went through. My father had kept out of the troughs. After all, he had the graph. But he knew they existed, and he had come often enough to the edge, and looked over, to know just what the troughs were like.

I put the heavy books aside. Someone else could deal with them. I hadn't the heart to burn the *Young Man with an Oil-Can*, it would have been like putting a match to the National Gallery. And who knows, my father's graph might still be of use to someone. 1994 is a long way off. The years between are not all lows.

Beside such weighty objects, the picture of a cocky twelve-year-old in glasses that never belonged to him is a very small affair, a private joke illustrating nothing but itself.

"It's all lies," Johnno would say. And in the end, perhaps, it is. Johnno's false disguise is the one image of him that has lasted, and the only one that could have jumped out from the page and demanded of me these few hours of my attention. Maybe, in the end, even the lies we tell define us. And better, some of them, than our most earnest attempts at the truth.